Superficial And Relative

A Collection

Daniel F. Creeden Jr

Special thanks to everyone who has ever put up with my nonsense: Kaitlyn, Mom, Dad, Zach, Erik, Snuffy, Al, Little Moe with the Gimpy leg, Cheeks, Boney Bob, Flip, I could go on forever baby!

"You were not there for the beginning. You will not be there for the end. Your knowledge of what is going on can only be superficial and relative."
                    -William S. Burroughs, Naked Lunch

Table of Contents

Superficial
and
Relative

Simulation

Hospitals tend to be cold places, both physically and emotionally. Physically, I like to think that they're kept cold in order to maintain a refrigeration effect: The lower the temperature, the longer it takes for the meat to go bad. Emotionally, I think it's a little more complex. A little bedside manner can go a long way in forcing you to forget how callous the whole healthcare process can be. A kind smile from a nurse or a bad joke from a doctor does its job most of the time, distracting you from whatever it is that has you in the hospital in the first place. A quick distraction to get your mind off of the fact that you are being poked and prodded through every orifice imaginable as a preventative means to keep you alive for another week before you find yourself back on one of their beds with a needle in your arm and a finger in your asshole.

But not all hospitals are the same.

Some are more like prisons.

Endless corridors of dirty white walls, ancient tile floors, caged up windows, and locked doors leading to rooms you're never allowed to see; that's the kind of hospital I'm in. The kind of hospital that keeps you trapped inside its walls, waving off any comparison to prison by lying to you and saying that it's all for your own good. They claim that keeping you separated from society at large is good for you; it can give you a chance to sit back and relax and reflect on whatever it is that has you locked up here in the first place.

That's bullshit, of course.

They didn't put us here for our own good, they put us here for society's good. By forcing us behind the walls of a mental institution and plying us with all the medication we can handle without falling to the floor and foaming at the mouth, they have effectively separated us from society as a whole and simply forgotten about the countless nights we have sat up and screamed out to the darkness and begged for someone to help us.

Besides, do you know how hard it is to relax in a mental institution? That's what they say they put us here for, right? To relax. Well you try and relax when you are surrounded by deranged individuals, half of whom aren't even aware of where they are. In their heads, they're still sitting wherever they were on the day their mind's got away from them, screaming out in fear of whatever trauma forced them into the state they find themselves in. The other half seem to be living in fear of the screamers.

The third half seems to know the truth. We recognize our situation and the absurdity of our own existence and we accept it as best we can. We sit and wait for a resolution that we are fully aware will never come.

None of it matters though. At the end of the day, I'm here for a reason. Everyone else in this hospital is completely inconsequential. The patients, the doctors, the orderlies, they are all meaningless because the reality is that none of them even exist.

That's why I'm here, in this prison they call a hospital. Because I figured it all out. Nothing is real. It's all an elaborate simulation set up inside of my mind. The building, the people in it, the walls outside, the trees beyond, the sky, the sun, the stars, everything is little more than a series of ones and zeros spelling out their own individual commands and forming a false reality for me to live in.

I don't think I was ever supposed to figure it out.

But here we are, sitting in the facade of a psychiatrist's office in a mental institution, lighting a cigarette and waiting for an exercise in meaninglessness to begin.

This place is brilliantly rendered, if I do say so myself. The way the smoke from my cigarette flourishes about the room, nestling itself amongst the numerous books sitting on the many bookshelves that surround the good doctors desk is mesmerizing. The way it manages to dance its way towards the ceiling and out through the vent high up on the roof is just so well made. I don't think my feeble brain could ever really comprehend the complexity that goes into programming such a thing, but I doubt that the subject is ever going to present itself to me. I was never supposed to figure it all out, remember?

"We talk about this every week," Dr. Frances says, breaking the silence that always seems to permeate through the opening minutes of our meetings, "You aren't allowed to smoke in here."

"Oh come on Doc," I answer after taking another deep drag from the Parliament Light that's burning between my fingers, "I thought that was just for group sessions."

"Nope." She replies, holding out an ash tray in my direction, "If I make an exception for you I'll need to make one for everyone else. You aren't special Frank."

"Oh come now," I say with a smirk, "We both know that isn't true."

"Go on. Put it out."

After one last drag I snuff out the cigarette in the ash tray. It's like this every week. It feels like a battle of wills, but really, it's all just a show. I'm just playing along with what she's asking of me while she is simply running out whatever complex subroutine the simulation has laid out for her. She doesn't know that of course. Most of the simulation is completely unaware that it's a part of it. It makes sense, a simulation that's self aware isn't going to fool anyone into thinking it's real and isn't that the whole point? The simulation, every part of it needs to know, for a fact, that what it is and how it works constitutes reality. It only works if the idea of its existence existing in any form other than the one it's presenting is simply waved away with a declaration of mental instability.

"Why do you even have an ash tray?"

"Because sometimes I have to deal with petulant patients who insist that the rules don't apply to them."

As she opens one of the many drawers on her desk and places the ash tray inside I stand up from my seat and walk to the window.

"It really is beautiful." I say, looking out passed the walls of the hospital in the distance, "I cant fathom the kind of processing power it takes to replicate it all so perfectly."

"The world is indeed a beautiful place."

"When I'm looking at it, sure."

"What do you mean?"

"Well," I say as I turn away from the window to face Dr. Frances, "If this was all created for me, you know, a simulation for me to exist in, then it only actually exists when I'm experiencing it, right?"

"You have to explain it to me Frank, I don't know how it all works."

"Of course," I say with a smile, "The simulation can't know how it works, that might ruin the whole thing."

"You said that nothing can exist if you aren't experiencing it." Dr. Frances says as she begins scratching out notes onto her clipboard, "Can you explain that to me?"

"Tell me doctor," I say as I turn my attention back out the window, "What is the only truth that anyone can really know?"

"The only truth?"

"Nothing in the universe is certain. Supposedly you're sitting behind me right now, scribbling notes onto a piece of paper about what you think you're learning from me. I can hear your pen scratching against the paper, I can smell your perfume, I can feel your presence in this room right now. For all intents and purposes, I'm experiencing your presence. I can't see you of course, I'm facing away, but all of the clues that I just laid out are right there, informing me of your presence."

"You can smell my perfume from all the way over there?"

"I can," I laugh in response, "It isn't too strong, but it's pleasant so it stands out."

"I see."

"But it's ephemeral. All of it. As soon as I put it out of my head, it all goes away. And that begs the question: If it can all go away so quickly and so easily, was it ever really there in the first place? Sure, I can turn around right now and see you sitting there behind me with my own eyes and confirm your presence for myself, but can I really trust my own eyes?"

"Why wouldn't you be able to trust your own eyes, Frank?"

"Because my eyes don't actually see anything!" I turn to look at Dr. Frances, "Sure, there you are, sitting at your desk, scribbling onto your clipboard, listening intently, but it isn't actually my eyes that are seeing you, is it?"

"Is it?"

"Nope!" I smile as I cross the room and sit down in the chair across from Dr. Frances, "My brain is what actually sees you. I'm told that my eyes absorb all the light out there and send signals into my head for my brain to interpret. How can I be sure that the way my brain is interpreting the world around me is true to the way the world exists?"

"That's a tough question Frank."

"And that, Doc, is where truth comes in."

"What do you mean?"

"The way my brain interprets the world is the only truth that I can possibly know. It's the only thing that informs me that I actually exist. It's impossible for me to know if you exist without actually experiencing things from your point of view. Therefore, as far as I know, you don't actually exist. The only way I can experience you is through all of the filters that have been put in place to force me to think that I'm experiencing you. You only exist within my own experience."

"But I'm experiencing you Frank, right now. I can see you, hear you, smell you, if I wanted to I could feel you. If we can both experience eachother, can't we then confirm that we both exist?"

"All that would confirm is that my brain is able to inform me that you believe that you exist. Your belief that you exist still only exists inside of my own head. The only confirmation of your own existence can come from within."

"So you don't believe that anything exists other than yourself?"

"No, of course not." I reply, again standing up from my seat, "Everything *exists*."

"If everything exists, then why can't you accept my confirmation of my own existence?"

"Everything exists inside of my head." I pull a book from one of the many bookshelves around the room, "This book, its cover, all of its pages, its musty smell, the ink forming the words on its pages, it's all right here in my hand. I can feel it, I can smell it, I can see it, if I read it

I might be able to understand it, but the only reason I can do any of that is because my brain tells me that I can. My brain is telling me that I'm standing here holding a book who's contents could teach me all I need to know about," I look at the book's cover and smile, "Existentialism: From Dostoevsky to Sartre. Hell of a book to randomly pull from the shelf, don't you think?"

"I have a lot of books up there."

"Of course." I smile as I examine the book a little closer and flip through its pages.

"So tell me, Frank," Dr. Frances looks up at me, "That book, what happens if you read it?"

"This particular book?" I ask, holding the book up, "I suppose I would learn a little something about existentialism."

"But how can you learn anything from it?" She asks, "If that book and everything written in it only exists in your mind, then how can you *learn* anything from it?"

"That is a great question, Doc." I say with a smile as I look over the books on her shelf.

"How is it possible to learn something that you already know?"

"Have you read all of these?" I ask, turning the subject away from her question.

"I have." She answers, "I had to."

"You had to?"

"College coursework isn't as easy as some people might think." She laughs to herself.

"There are a lot of philosophy books up here," I say as I look over the shelves, "Do psychologists usually take an interest in philosophy?"

"If we want to understand how the mind works, then we need to understand how to question what we know about it."

"Well put."

"Frank, you didn't answer my question," Dr. Frances says as she adjusts her position in her seat, turning the conversation back to where I had left it, "How can you learn something that you already know?"

"Do you know what Plato thought about knowledge?"

"Enlighten me."

With a smile I pull a book from the shelf and hand it to Dr. Frances.

"I thought you said you read all of these."

"I have." She replies with a sigh as she takes the book from me and examines the cover, "But it's been some time since I've cracked open Meno and Phaedo Frank."

"I'm teasing!" I answer with a smug laugh, "But they *are* fascinating. Something I would recommend picking up and thumbing through once in a while."

"I'll keep that in mind." She says as she sets the book down on her desk and goes back to scratching down notes.

"Well, whenever you do," I say, sitting back down in the seat across from Dr. Frances, "You'll see that Plato had some very interesting thought's about learning."

"Is that so?"

"Plato believed that we are all born possessing all knowledge and that our realization of that knowledge is only contingent on our discovery of it."

"The doctrine of recollection."

"Indeed."

"So you believe that you already know everything written in all of these books," She gestures around the room, "You just need to read them to realize what you already knew."

"Exactly."

"Okay," She scribbles down another line in her notes, "So if this were the case then you already posses all of the knowledge of the universe."

"That's right."

"How did it get there?" She looks up from her notes, "How did you come into possession of all the knowledge of the universe?"

"That's the big question, now isn't it?"

"I'm sorry?"

"Listen," I say, "We've gone over what I believe a thousand times. We both know that it's an exercise in futility. I'm going to tell you that I'm living within a simulation, that everything around me, you included, is an elaborate fabrication placed directly into my brain in order to placate me and keep me submissive to whatever it is I am being used for on the outside. You already know that I know the truth, but because you're just another part of what exists in my head, you can't ever bring yourself to realize that I'm right. You want to know how I came into possession of all the knowledge of the universe? It's because the universe only exists within my own head! It's all just a matter of tapping into it and understanding that what I know is all that really matters."

"If your own knowledge is all that really matters, then what exactly is the point to all of this? Why are you here?"

"That depends on what you mean by here. Here in this room? Here in this hospital? Here in the simulation? Here in my head?"

"Here can mean whatever you want it to mean."

"Well," I begin, "I suppose I am here because this is where I'm supposed to be."

"What do you mean?"

"Even though everything only exists my mind, I don't actually have control over it. I may think I understand it, but I'm forever stuck under the thumb of the simulation. I'm forced to live the way it want's me to live."

"So you retain all of the knowledge of the universe, but you have no free will?"

"I have free will."

"But you just said that you are forced to live the way the simulation want's you to live."

"I still have free will."

"How can you have free will if you're own existence remains contingent on the wills of the simulated universe that you believe you're stuck inside?"

"There's a difference between freedom and free will Dr. Frances, and I think you already understand that."

"Well according to you, I understand everything you understand."

"But can you recollect my knowledge?"

"I can if I'm you."

"...Perhaps"

"If my existence only exists in your mind, then I'm just you, right?"

"You're simulated in my head."

"So my existence is reliant on your existence. We're two existences intertwined in a way where one can't exist without the other."

"No." I say, preventing her from going on, "We talked about this before. Your existence exists *because* mine exists. Your existence is reliant on mine, but my existence can still exist without yours."

"But we just agreed that if I exist within you, then I'm a part of you. If I'm a part of the universal knowledge that you possess, then you can't exist without me. You said it yourself, what you know is all that really matters. You know me, therefore I am part of what matters. You can't exist without me."

"I can!" I bark back, "If I can leave the simulation, then you'll no longer exist."

"But how do you know that you can exist outside of the simulation?" Dr. Frances asks, "That is to say, if you truly are living within a simulation and you can somehow escape it, how do you know that you exist out there?"

"The only truth I know is that I exist." I answer, "I can only experience the world from my own perspective."

"But how do you know that your own perspective is truth?" She asks, "What if outside of this simulation you find yourself in another simulation where *you're* the elaborate construct sitting behind a desk listening to the subject of the simulation laboriously explaining how their own existence is the only real existence?"

"If I'm experiencing it then I know that it's true."

"But I'm experiencing the world right now and you can't accept that as truth, so why can you accept your own?"

"Because it's all I know."

"Perhaps you have more to learn," Dr. Frances replies, "more to understand."

I sit back and think on this for a moment. I'm not wrong, the subjectivity of my own experience being all I can understand is an objective fact. I can't experience you just like you can't experience me. Two minds can never truly know eachother, no matter how often they trick themselves into thinking that their connections run deeper than is humanly possible.

"There is always more to understand, Doctor." I smile, "But there is never any way to test it."

"What do you mean?"

"Well," I reply, "If I want to try and understand what my reality is like beyond the simulation, I need to escape it."

"The simulation?"

"Exactly. The only way for me to understand what reality is like beyond the one I know right now is to experience it on that level, outside of the facade in front of me."

"How might you do that?" Dr. Frances asks, frantically writing more notes onto her clipboard. She knows what comes next.

"I'd have to shut down the simulation." I smile, "I would have to end all of existence."

"How can you end all of existence Frank?"

"Existence as I know it only exists within my own head." My smile washes away, "So I suppose the only way to end existence is to kill myself."

"That's a little drastic, don't you think?"

"Not at all. If everything only exists in my own head, then nothing can exist without me. It's the only logical way to escape the simulation. By shutting it down."

"What makes you think that killing yourself within a simulation will have any effect on what happens outside of it?"

"I have no idea how it works." I laugh, "All I know is that by ending my own existence, I end my own experience. If there is something more beyond my experience, I would love to find out. If not, oh well, my experience will be over and there's nothing more to be done. I'll have managed to escape either way."

"I don't think killing yourself is a good idea." Dr. Frances says as she finishes adding more to her notes.

"It's not like it matters," I reply, "The simulation isn't going to let me kill myself."

"No." Dr. Frances says, "I suppose not."

"That's why you exist. You're here as one of the many safeguards put in place to keep the simulation running. You declare me unstable and place me into an asylum where you can watch me twenty four hours a day, effectively imprisoning me in my own head keeping the whole thing going. Forever and ever."

"Then why are we here?"

"Do we need to define *here* again Doc?" I ask with a laugh.

"If my part of your simulation is to keep you from shutting the whole thing down, then why are we even here talking? What's the point? Why don't we just lock you away somewhere where you can't harm yourself and forget about you and let the simulation play out without you?"

"I honestly don't know, Doctor."

"Oh, so we finally found something you don't know."

"No," I say with a smile, "It's just something I've yet to recollect."

"Of course." Dr. Frances says as she jots down one last note.

"Well," I say, looking up at the clock on the wall, "I think it's safe to say we've hit our wall today."

"I'm sorry?" Dr. Frances asks, looking up from her notes, "We still have another twenty minutes."

"We've hit our wall today Doc. I think we're done for the day."

"But I think I have more to learn from you, so I can help you."

"But I've nothing more to give."

"Why is that?"

"I'm tired, Doc." I say with a sigh, "I'm getting tired of telling you the same thing every day and going nowhere. You and I both know that these sessions are doing nothing to help me."

"But I want to help you." She answers, "I honestly believe that if I listen to you more…"

"You can't help me." I smile, "No matter how hard you try."

"But I truly believe I can. I refuse to believe that anybody is beyond hope."

"How can you help me if you aren't even real?"

"Frank, listen, I…"

"I'm tired Doc. Can we please just call it a day?"

"Well if you're tired, I suppose there's no use in trying to push it."

"Same time tomorrow?" I ask.

"Same time tomorrow." She replies, pressing the button on the intercom system sitting on her desk, "Frank is done here, could you please have the orderlies escort him back to his room."

As the door opens and the orderlies step in, I stand up from my seat and quietly go along with them. I head back to my room where I can sit in silence for the foreseeable future. The white walls of my room are a stark reminder that anything beyond them holds a questionable existence that's entirely dependent on my own perception of how it all works.

Is Dr. Frances still sitting in her office, going over her days notes on me and planning out how the future of my therapy will play out, or is the space where her office had sat only moment's ago occupied by the eternal blackness of what lies beyond my understanding? Is there anything passed these walls in front of me, or do they simply represent a barrier between myself and the oblivion beyond? Does the world behind me even exist if I'm not looking at it?

Does any of it exist?

Do I even exist?

I suppose I'll never truly know.

Tobin the Dog Man

Weekends meant nothing to Tobin. Sure, they were a reprieve from the mundane workweek that had its cold hard strangle wrapped firmly around his ladylike neck, but to a man like Tobin, one who held nothing but a silent misanthropic distaste for his fellow man, the weekends simply meant forty eight hours of silent contemplation.

Tobin had one single friend in his life. One friend to whom he was willing to confide in when he was feeling down. Someone to whom he could impart his deepest darkest secrets. A friend to whom his words which he had kept held back and tucked away from any and every other human being on the planet were spoken freely and openly. This friend's name was Danke-Schoen. A small white and tan Bichon-Frise who despite his penchant for administering wet dog kisses up and down any face within a two foot radius did a bang up job at keeping his mouth shut and holding onto Tobin's secrets.

"It's almost time, Danke-Schoen." Tobin said while glancing down at his watch.

Danke-Schoen brimmed with pride, ecstatic that Tobin had spoken to him.

"Your friends should start arriving soon," Tobin said with an uncharacteristic smile, "This party's gonna be POPPIN!"

Danke-Schoen's tail began to wag.

Tobin sat silently staring at Danke-Schoen in a way that could only be described as creepy. He stared into Danke-Schoen's waiting eyes and took in every subtle movement that came from his eager dog face and interpreted them as he saw fit. For the most part, these movements were positive. Danke-Schoen was clearly happy with his life and loved Tobin and being around him. Other times, Tobin saw something that got him thinking. A nervous glance away or a subtle nostril flare betrayed Danke-Schoen's secret emotions to Tobin. The ones that Danke-Schoen preferred to keep secret. His secret judgments. At times, Tobin felt he could pick up on the acute sense of contemptuousness that Danke-Schoen hid deep inside. These thoughts have a bad habit of causing a silent, internal rage within Tobin but he has always been good about not letting that rage out. He had come up with his own special way of dealing with it. Without breaking eye contact, Tobin slowly reached into his breast pocket and pulled out a small notepad and a sharpie pen. He looked down at the notepad and with an angry look on his face, Tobin wrote something down. He looked up at Danke-Schoen, and with a grin he showed him what he had written on the notepad.

'Fuck you'

Danke-Schoen's tail began wagging wildly, once again excited by the fact that his master was paying him some sort of attention, and Tobin sneered at his secret knowledge that Danke-Schoen, a young gullible dog, was indeed unable to read.

In English at least.

As Tobin sat smiling in a dense cloud of satisfaction, content in his handling of Danke-Schoen's ill tempered thoughts, he was startled by the sudden introduction of the blaring ring of a doorbell into the peaceful silence that Tobin's chosen lifestyle brought about. Tobin tucked his notepad back into his breast pocket and stood up from his chair.

"They're heeeeere!" Tobin sung to Danke-Schoen's delight.

Tobin rushed to the door, narrowly avoiding a run in between his shin and the corner of the coffee table. He glanced back at Danke-Schoen before turning the doorknob and greeting his esteemed guests.

"Hey Tobin." Came the voice of Marta, a coworker of Tobin's.

Marta, a lovely young woman, dressed to the nines, was standing on Tobin's porch. In her hand she held the looped end of a somewhat lengthy canvas leash. At the end of the leash stood Bingo, a tan Great Dane who stood three feet tall at the shoulder and maintained a stupid dog like smile, his tongue hanging stupidly from the side of his big stupid mouth.

"Hello, Marta." Tobin responded, refusing to look her in the face.

"Listen," Marta said, "Are you sure about this? I mean I really appreciate you looking after Bingo, but are you sure you wouldn't rather come along with me to the office party? Everyone would be happy to see you there."

"Oh, no," Tobin answered, refusing to take his eyes away from Bingo, "Bingo here isn't the only one of my co-worker's dogs that I agreed to watch tonight."

"That's a shame." Marta said with a bit of a frown, "I was kind of hoping I could get you to come with me..."

"Yea, well," Tobin said as bent down to greet Bingo, "We don't always get what we want."

"Too bad." Marta sighed as she handed Bingo's leash off to Tobin, "I'll see you later on tonight when I pick him up. Have a nice evening Tobin."

"Uh huh." Tobin grunted as he led Bingo into the house and closed the door behind him leaving Marta alone on the porch.

Over the next twenty or so minutes, Tobin was visited by somewhere between sixteen and twenty two different co-workers, all dropping off dogs and heading out to attend an office party. Tobin was introduced to an English Bulldog named Chesterfield, a Greyhound named Enzo, a Basset Hound named Jimbo, and a broad menagerie of other dogs, all both upset at the sudden disappearance of their owners and still excited to get to hang out with a whole new batch of friends.

After the final dog had arrived, Tobin turned to take in his living room. The dogs were absolutely everywhere. In the living room, in the kitchen, on the couches, everywhere Tobin looked, there was a dog. Tobin looked over the situation and he smiled.

"Well," Tobin said, addressing the dogs, "I'll give you all some space."

Tobin smiled again, content in the fact that his normally silent and boring living room was now absolutely filled with life. He lamented the fact that, eventually, all the dogs would be gone, but regardless of this fact, Tobin felt a warm glow rise from deep inside his chest and fill him with the kind of happiness that only a house full of dogs could bring about.

"Oh," Tobin started, turning back to address the dogs, "Try not to have TOO much fun, alright? We want you guys coming back in the future?"

Tobin headed down the hall and into his room. He lay down onto his bed, crossed his legs and threw his arms behind his head as he closed his eyes and let his consciousness drown itself into the sound of twenty some odd dogs enjoying their night in his living room. He fell asleep, contented by the fact that he was making a significant difference in the lives of these dogs. Tobin was happy that the dogs were happy.

In the living room the dogs sniffed about, pissing and shitting everywhere and humping to exert dominance as dogs are wont to do.

All was good in the world.

Wake
(Journal Entry c. 2015)

The sun rises on yet another day.

The light creeps its way through my curtains and blinds me through my eyelids, beckoning me awake and forcing me to yet again face another day filled with nothing.

My dreams in the night always seem to hold the same theme. Drowning in a world where I don't want to be; the walls collapsing onto me but never quite crushing me; a secret pistol finding its way into my hands and begging me to end it all.
The light pulls me away from this sense of rampant loathing and forces reality onto me. A reality full of foggy thoughts, a body that refuses to work properly, and an all around sense of unaccompanied discomfort. We're supposed to find calm in the light of reality. We're supposed to find comfort. Compared to the dream-state it pulls me from, I suppose the waking world is the one I'd rather be in. But that feeling of drowning, the feeling of the walls collapsing on top of me, at least that is something. At least I can feel something in the horrifying state that it represents.

In the real world, I can barely even feel my fingers.

We Just Found Out That This Guy Has Cancer

Every day I wake up and find a new reason to hate myself.

Not necessarily in the "Life sucks, I want to kill myself" kind of way, although those days do happen, but in more of a "How in the fuck do I go on living inside of a body that doesn't seem to want me in it?" sort of way.

I don't dislike the person that I am. I'm a delight, if I do say so myself. I am always trying my best to look on the bright side of things, trying to inject as much positivity into the world as I can. I'd like to think that it helps to counteract all of the negativity that the modern world seems to put out, but that's a pretty steep hill to overcome. A simple drop of goodness in an ocean of negative interactions.

Everyday spent in this modern world is a day spent being bombarded with negativity. Everywhere you look someone is trying to bring you down. I was talking to a neighbor just the other day and he thought that I would like to know about how his dog was just diagnosed with dog cancer.

My dog loves going out for walks. Most dogs do, really. He sees me pick up his leash and he is sent into a fit of hysterics, running all over the house and spinning around in circles like a psychopath, prompted entirely by the prospect of getting to roam around the neighborhood for a little while sniffing at other dogs piss puddles and covering them up with a bit of his own.

I wish there was a way for me to feel such unabashed joy for something so simple and disgusting.

Anyway, I pick up the leash and send the dog into hysterics before strapping on his harness and heading out the front door.

As we make our way down the driveway, before we even make it to the sidewalk, we are greeted by a man who lives on our block. An older gentleman, somewhere in his mid sixties, walking his dog. Some sort of mid sized mixed breed mutt who although is somewhat diminutive in stature, still dwarfs my tiny little dog.

"Good morning!" I say with a smile that is oozing with a positive attitude.

"Morning!" He says, returning the smile.

My dog has always been somewhat timid around other dogs. He won't go out of his way to greet them, but he also won't run away when greeted. The man's dog greeted mine in the way that dogs are wont to do. By sniffing his asshole.

My dog returns the favor and the two are new friends.

"How old is he?" The man asks.

"Six years old." I reply, "I've had him since he was a puppy."

"Oh, so he is fully grown then?" He asks.

It might seem like a rude question, in a very abstract sort of way, but it isn't. My dog is less than five pounds. To say he's a runt is an understatement.

"Yep!" I reply, "He's been fully grown since he was just a couple weeks old!"

"Wow," He said with a smile, "We just found out that this guy has cancer."

It was like he could sense the happiness I got out of talking about my dog and decided that he needed to remind me that life is fleeting. That at the drop of a hat, something can befall us and throw our lives into upheaval.

That isn't to say that I am not familiar with that kind of thing.

When I was diagnosed with MS, my life was thrown upside down. Literally, at certain points. On the day that I finally decided to go to the hospital, as I was walking into the emergency room, I found myself "walking" at one moment, and lying flat on my back the next. Then a few hours later lying in a hospital bed with a flashy new yellow wristband with the words FALL RISK written on it in bold black letters.

This is a huge part of the reason why I find it increasingly difficult to try and spread positivity and wake up hating myself in different ways everyday.

MS is a gift that simply refuses to stop giving, and there's no cure for its generosity.

Dizziness here, random pains there, numbness aplenty, all turning up randomly on any given day, reminding me that I am not normal anymore. A slap in the face every morning coupled with a screaming internal voice telling me that things will never be like they were.

Creekside Dummies

A pair of turkey vultures circle high above the fields of golden grass that cover the hills of Garin Regional Park. Their flight pattern is constant as they watch and wait for their bounty to collapse under the heat of the California sun. Their determination is admirable, but it's all in vain, for the two young men descending the access road that connects the elevated area surrounding Jordan Pond with the wooded canyon down below don't seem to be in any sort of peril. Death is far from eminent, but with teenagers, you never know.

"Tommy, you retard," Louis barked, his voice echoing throughout the canyon below, "you can't eat your own tongue."

"Yes you can!" Tommy replied with excitement, "It happened to my cousin Mark's friend. He did a bunch of oxy and couldn't feel his mouth. When he tried to eat his dinner, he accidentally chewed his tongue off and swallowed it."

"So what, he didn't notice the blood in his mouth?" Asked Louis.

"No," Tommy answered, "he took so many pain killers that he couldn't *feel* anything!"

"Yea, but what about all the fucking blood that had to have been pouring out of his face?" Louis asked as they reached the bottom of the hill and entered the small meadow that acted as a foyer for the wooded area where they were headed, "What, was he just shoveling food into his mouth and not noticing the blood pouring out?"

"Louis, don't be an idiot. Tongues don't bleed." Tommy said, matter-of-factly.

There was a moment of silence as Louis waited and tried to fully comprehend exactly what Tommy had just said to him.

"Are you fucking kidding me Tom?" Louis replied, turning to face Tommy.

"No man, I'm serious! I bite my tongue all the time and it never bleeds." Tommy answered, stopping next to Louis.

"Tommy, tongues *absolutely* bleed! What do you think are in the giant veins on the bottom of them?" Louis said, opening his mouth and pointing out the highly visible veins on the bottom of his tongue.

"Spit."

"What?"

"Yea, they carry the spit into your tongue. That's why your mouth is always wet."

"Has the public school system really failed you this badly?"

A moment of silence passed as Tommy tried to understand exactly what it was that Louis was saying. A wave of realization washed over him and he understood.

"Are you calling me stupid?"

The two hurriedly entered the shaded canopy of the woods. They followed along the familiar path, one they have walked on a nearly daily basis for close to a year, as it snaked along the small creek bed that had run dry earlier in the summer. As the creek rounded dramatically towards a wall of earth, the path continued on, turning into a long unstable wooden bridge that stretched for around a hundred feet, crossing to the other side.

"Tommy, I'm not calling you stupid." Louis said as he crossed the bridge. "I'm just saying that you seem to be grossly misinformed about a few things."

"I'm not misinformed." Tommy said, waiting for Louis to cross the bridge before stepping onto it himself.

"Why do you always do that?" Louis asked, looking back and watching Tommy step onto the bridge.

"Because look at this thing," Tommy answered, motioning to the bridge underneath him, "it's never going to hold both of our weight."

"Better safe than sorry, I guess." Louis replied, "But listen, who told you that the veins under your tongue carry saliva into your mouth?"

"No one told me, I just sort of figured it out." Tommy answered, rushing across the bridge.

"See? That's not how it works!" Louis said with a hint of anger in his voice, "School's supposed to teach you how these sort of things work! Not just force you to try and figure it out on your own, letting you honestly believe that the asinine reasoning that your brain somehow came up with is the way it works."

"Sorry Lou," Tommy said as the two continued along the path, "But it really sounds like you're calling me stupid."

"Trust me Tommy, I'm not."

"All right then," Tommy said with a smile, "I guess I'll just have to believe you."

The two walked left at the fork in the path, towards a boulder, bedazzled with graffiti from former low lives that passed through here long ago. They followed the path until it intersected with the creek, no bridge this time. A large branch extended outward over the path with the words "BEE-RAY" deeply carved into it which the two touched as they passed under, breaking away from the path and now walking down the rocky creek bed. They followed it along as it curved around a corner and out of sight from the path.

Over the years, the creek had carved away the earth beneath a massive oak tree creating a large natural overhang that acted as refuge from the weather, no matter the time of year. A tiny pond created a natural end to the creek bed before it started again on the other side. The large oak hung overhead, encapsulating the area in a dome-like fashion with two plastic chairs sitting alongside a folding card table, all positioned nicely under the overhang where the two sat down and settled in. The roots from the tree overhead cut through the ground and hung from the ceiling of the friends' humble abode, occasionally dropping bits of grime down onto the table.

"I told you we should get something to cover this stuff up." Tommy said as he lifted his chair and shook off the grime.

"Is it really that hard to clean it off?" Louis responded as he cleared the table clean with a single swipe of his arm. "It would take more time clearing off the cover than it would to just wipe it off, and time isn't something we want to waste in a time like this."

"What do you mean a time like this?"

"I mean, why should we waste time cleaning when we can be spending that time getting nice and high!" Louis answered as he pulled a small baggie of pot out of his jacket pocket.

"Oh shit." Tommy said, quietly, but loud enough for Louis to hear.

"What is it?" Louis asked.

"I left my pipe in my locker."

"Don't worry about it, I got us covered." Louis pulled a small glass pipe out from his pocket with a smile.

"No, I figured you would have brought one Lou, I was just really looking forward to breaking in my new baby. Did I show it to you?"

"Yea, during every break at school today."

"Hah, yea, I'm just so proud of the little guy."

"Is proud really an emotion you should be having for a pipe?"

"I've never had one before. It's kind of like my pride and joy! It's shiny and black, with…"

"…A hand painted Dragon along the side, and it looks like he is holding the bowl," Louis interrupted, as if he had heard the speech before, "I know, you told me."

"Sorry Lou."

"No worries man, but just put it out of your mind, cause we aren't going back for it. We'll just use it tomorrow."

"Right on."

Louis set his pipe, green with a black swirling pattern, onto the table and set the small baggy next to it. He grabbed the closest chair he could find and pulled it close to himself. After a quick brush off, Louis was seated and hunched over the pipe, loading up their daily duties.

Tommy, not one to sit patiently, made his way over to the pond that sat just west of their smoking setup. He knelt down to look into the water and gazed at the large tadpoles swimming fruitlessly near the surface.

"Hey Lou, check this out, Tadpoles!"

"I'm a little busy over here Tom, and maybe if you would settle down a bit, you'd be busy too." Louis said as he blew out a large billow of smoke into the air above him. "It's your hit, get over here before I pass you over."

"Shit man, I paid too, that's just as much my weed as it is yours!" Tommy said in a panic as he hustled over to the table, "It's just that I've never seen tadpoles before! They had legs on them, that's fucking cool!"

"Settle down, there!" Louis handed Tommy the pipe and he quickly joined in on the fun.

***

"Listen…" Tommy said.

"Listen to wha…?"

"SHHHH! Just listen."

After about 30 seconds or so of silence, Louis decided to break it.

"There is nothing to listen to you psychopath!"

"That's the point asshole! Just listen to the silence! It's beautiful!"

"No, Garfunkel, silence is just proof that you're alone. You want beautiful, I'll give you beautiful."

As if he had conjured some sort of magical spell, Louis turned in his chair and lifted himself out of it, and in one fell swoop, dropped his pants and sent a loud, long fart heading towards poor Tommy's dopey face.

"That's fucked up man! What the hell is wrong with you?!?"

Just then, the two heard a loud rustle, as if something had fallen over, just around the bend on the other side of the pond where the tadpoles lived.

"Oh shit… What the hell was that?" Tommy asked, visibly shaken.

"I don't know, but it sounded big…" Answered Louis, "Let's go see."

"Are you crazy? What if it's a mountain lion?"

"What if it is? It's headed this way, so we're dead either way." Louis answered, jovially.

"Seriously Lou, let's get out of here!"

"Tommy, stop being such a little bit…"

Louis's insult was interrupted by the sudden appearance of a large female deer and her fawn as they came hurriedly around the corner, through the water and off in the distance.

"Holy shit!" Tommy screamed.

"It's just a couple of deer you chicken shit." Louis answered through his laughter.

"Yea, but why are they running?" Tommy asked, still scared.

"Maybe it's a mountain lion." Louis joked.

"You think?"

"No, I don't think! They were running! That's what deer do! They run all over the fucking planet! Just calm the fuck down!"

As if his words were some sort of cue, the two witnessed several bright flashes of light, accompanied by a loud buzzing sound.

"Explain that Lou!" Tommy shouted.

"Well, that was obviously a…"

Louis's explanation was immediately interrupted by a thunderous boom, knocking the two off of their feet and onto their asses. As fast as he could, Tommy got to his feet and began to run, while Louis gave chase.

"Tommy, stop!"

"Fuck you man! I ain't staying anywhere near that shit!"

"Tommy, seriously, come back!"

"No fucking way Lou, I am out of…"

Tommy's gripe was shortened by Louis's tackle, taking the two to the ground. Tommy, unhindered, tried to scurry away from Louis's grip, but it was to no avail.

"Louis, let me go!"

"Tommy, Listen!"

"No, I am not going to get abducted and have my asshole probed by some sick alien pervert!"

"Tommy, that isn't going to happen! Just shut the fuck up and listen!"

"What?"

"SHHHH!"

Tommy decided to calm himself down a bit and the two sat silently, listening for any sound. Nothing seemed to come.

"Lou, dude, what are we doing, what are we listening for?"

"Tommy, just…"

Just then, the two heard some rustling as a large turkey vulture leapt from the brush and flew high into the tree above them. It sat in the boughs of a large oak tree, preening its black feathers and occasionally stopping to peer at the two scared young men with its beady yellow eyes. It stared deeply into them, not the inquisitive stare of an animal but as if it knew what it was staring at and as if it were feeding off of their fear.

"What the fuck is it doing Lou?"

"Its waiting."

"Waiting for what?"

"For us to die."

A sudden realization of the reality of what vultures are, scavengers of the dead, was cast over Tommy and he became visibly ill. His skin flushed and quickly turned a shade of green normally reserved for corpses. He started to notice a blackness at the edges of his vision and the slight twinkling of stars that weren't there. He felt himself begin to go faint just before he felt Louis' hand slap against his back. The stars went away, his vision cleared, he felt the blood rush back into his head, and he was suddenly aware of the laughter permeating the forest, the source of which was less than a foot to his left.

"The fuck are you laughing at!?"

"Your face! Oh my god! You look terrified! It isn't waiting for us to die, you fucking idiot, it's perching to get out of the rain!"

"It isn't raining! What the hell are you talking about?"

"Not yet, but it will be! Don't you smell it? I know you heard the thunder, it sent you running!"

"I… I guess I didn't notice…"

"Well, let's go, we don't want to get caught in a storm, not out here, not while we are high. I can barely stand the fact that we are going to have to walk back up that hill; I would hate to have to do it in the mud."

"Yea… Yea, let's get out of here…"

Phone Apps, Dating, and Eating Ass

First dates tend to be stressful for me. My low self esteem mixed with my crippling inability to impress the fairer sex tend to swirl themselves around in my head creating a delightful cocktail of anxiety and tension that manifests as a series of nervous twitches and an inability to speak properly.

At least now we have this menagerie of phone apps that set out to help us get around all this nervous tension. A misleading photo and a paragraph of text cut through all of the banal minutia of getting to know someone and put all of the cards out on the table.

We both know why we are here, sweetheart. I want to fuck and you want to suck some dick. We can help each other out here.

People helping people, that's the future of dating.

Of course, not many people will admit that. None of us want to come across as a sex crazed weirdo when we're directing our raging erections and sopping wet vaginas at these strangers on the internet. We all want to maintain some semblance of nuance in the situation.

Women can sense desperation and they know they are better than having to deal with that. For the most part, that is entirely acceptable. In the world of online dating, we are only as good as the people we have sex with. If someone decides to go slumming, they should hold no expectation of ever getting out of the slum-hole that they have created.

This is especially true for women. They are expected to turn down sex at every turn in an attempt to catch the sex crazed male of the species in their honey trap. Their end game, apparently, is to marry a man and then deprive him of sex for the rest of his life until he dies an unhappy, bitter old man.

Women like sex. It is all a part of the natural need to propagate the species and to pretend that they don't is not only ignorant, it is unacceptable. There is a reason nature stored all of those nerve endings inside of our dirty-sticks and fuck-holes. If sex didn't feel good, it would just be a disgusting display of fluid transfer that no one would ever want to deal with. Humans would be like pandas; facing extinction because of the mere fact that we couldn't be bothered to fuck each other.

The human mind is intelligent. So intelligent that without all those nerve endings to make our genitals feel a rush when we copulate and trick us into thinking that what we are doing is beautiful, we would recognize just how disgusting it all really is. Slamming our piss parts against each other until we leave a frothing mess on the sheets that one day might turn into a screaming ball of disgust that'll soon become a whole new person that will never really be able to function on its own.

Have you ever seen Eraserhead?

Never mind…

Companionship. That's all any of us really want; to find our own pack that we can howl at the moon with and never let anyone tell us to stop.

But that's not really what Tinder and Bumble and Grinder and all these nonsense phone apps are all about now, are they?

They aren't about companionship. Not in the long term at least. They're for living in the moment. They're there to help trick our stupid monkey brains into remembering that sex is nothing special. Just something we do to make our dicks and pussies feel nice.

I couldn't really tell you why I'm getting into all of this. Phone app dating is best left for the young. The current youthful generation where licking out an asshole is akin to a nice little hello.

It's all too fast paced for me.

I would much rather get to know someone. Learn about the ins and outs of who they are. Their hopes, their fears, everything that makes them the special individual that they seem to be. I want to build a relationship with someone over time and then one day be *allowed* to lick their butthole.

It's a weird world we live in where ass eating can be mentioned alongside first dates, but here we are.

In the 50's, a boy would take out his best girl with his endgame being that she will wear his varsity jacket to school and show it off to all her friends.

You go Moose, get that gal!

Now-a-days, a guy will put in as little effort as possible to get a drunk girl to take him into the bar bathroom and let him eat her shitter for fifteen minutes before parting ways and never seeing each other again.

I blame 9/11.

Lick out her asshole Johnny! Do it like a true patriot! Don't you DARE let the terrorists win!

I'm not sure where I was going with any of that.

 Sorry.

To those of us in our thirties, however, the world of online dating is something entirely different. Everyone wants sex, but not without a few caveats. The getting to know you process that I was lamenting before still exists. The women that I have met over the last few years have all been pretty straightforward about what they want. They want companionship. They want someone who can be there for them; someone who can be present for them when they really need it. Many of them needed me to understand that their children come first, before anything. As a father myself, I respect that. They want to know me and I want to know them.

Sex is in the backseat at this point in my life and it's nice to see that's true to others in similar situations.

I didn't do any dating in my twenties. My time was being spent raising my daughter. Now, with a sense of hindsight and the ability to look back at what I may or may not have missed out on during that time in my life I can genuinely say that I hold no ill will towards the world that I didn't get to participate in. But at the same time, I hold no desire to find out what could have been.

Modern dating is a kids game. Something that truly passed me by years ago. That isn't to say that it didn't help me to meet some nice, interesting people. All I'm saying is that the dating world is something that is now in my past and I am okay with that.

28

Maybe You Should Get a Cat

Karen's dog wanted nothing to do with her. No matter how many treats or hugs or kisses she gave to him he simply wouldn't have it. It wasn't her fault, dogs can be finicky. Sometimes all it takes is a small piece of ham from your sandwich to get them to love you forever with an unquestionable loyalty.

Those dogs would jump in front of a car for you.

Karen's dog would never do that.

"What's going on here?" Karen asked, "Do I smell?"

The dog refused to answer.

"That's it, isn't it? I smell bad. You don't want to be around me because I stink!"

Again, the dog refused to answer.

"Well let's see how you like this!" Karen shouted as she scampered passed the dog in a huff.

Karen made her way into the kitchen. She opened her refrigerator and pulled out a particularly large tupper-ware container and placed it down onto the counter. As she opened the container's lid to take a nice deep whiff of its contents, Karen shot the dog a cheeky look. A look that said 'Hey there fella, why don't you come on over here and see what mama's cookin?!'

The dog just licked its genitals.

In an apparent fit of anger, Karen jammed her fingers into the container and pulled out a rather large bit of hand cut ham. She flapped the ham around a bit in the dog's direction, hoping it would pick up on the scent. Karen took the ham and began to rub it vigorously onto herself, dousing her neck in ham stink. She wiped it onto her chest and onto her arms and into her armpits.

Keeping the ham in her hand, Karen began to make her way across the room. The dog finished licking its genitals and looked up, noticing Karen and her ham making their way towards it.

"What is this Karen?" The dog asked, "What are we doing here?"

"You want some HAM?" Karen said in her best fit of baby talk.

"I would love some ham, Karen." The dog responded stoically, "But not like this."

"Come get the ham!" Karen beckoned, "Do you smell it? Huh?!"

"Of course I smell it Karen." The dog answered matter-of-factly, "I'm a dog. We are world renowned for our sense of smell."

"THEN WHY WON'T YOU ACKNOWLEDGE ME?!" Karen shouted.

"To be honest, Karen, I just don't really like you." The dog retorted, "There's just something about you."

"Something about me?!" Karen repeated, "What about me?!"

"Oh Karen, don't take it so personally." The dog replied, "I'm just not a big fan of people."

"Dog's love people! It's your whole appeal!"

"Not all dogs, Karen. Not all dogs."

"Name me ONE dog that doesn't like people."

"Well, me, for one." The dog answered, "Then there's my friend Jerry. You know him, the poodle down the street."

"The Framingham's dog?!"

"I guess." The dog answered, "Listen, Karen, I tolerate you. You should take that as a compliment. Most dogs that don't like people won't even give them that much. You rubbed ham all over your neck in an effort to get me to come say hi. I appreciate that. I appreciate the effort. But the fact of the matter is that no matter what you do, no matter how hard you try, I will never like you. It's in my DNA."

"That's disheartening." Karen said, disappointed.

"Maybe you should get a cat."

Karen thought on this for a moment before being interrupted by the opening of the front door. It was Tad, Karen's husband, and he was coming home from work. As soon as Tad stepped in, the dog dashed across the room to meet him. It leaped through the air and was immediately greeted by a flurry of pets and pats from Tad.

"Tad, my goodness! Where have you been all day?!" The dog shouted.

As Tad continued to dole out pets and pats, the dog couldn't help but feel Karen's cold hard stare from across the room. He quickly jumped down from Tad.

"I... Um... I mean, hello, other human. I didn't miss you at all..."

Mexican Sorcery, the Only Explanation

The heat of the high noon sun beat down across Thomas Macarnold's strong broad shoulders. His blue cotton shirt soaked with sweat bore the markings of the previous months work, covered in white lines where the sweat had long since dried up. His jeans, caked in dust hung low over his hard bottomed boots, comfortably lined in calf's fur, making fifty two straight hours of panning in the heat of the California sun seem like fifty two straight hours of walking on a cloud. A cloud that holds onto every bit of the humid ninety five degree weather within, but a cloud none the less.

Normally, gold-panners would pay good money for the best piece of equipment they could get their hands on. Heavy pans made from iron seemed to be the norm, but Thomas had just spent most of his money on this vast plot of land, and his wife Clara spent what was left on a nice pair of boots for him to work in. As a compromise, he's spent the last few months prospecting for gold using a pie tin that has met the sharp end of a nail in a pair of boots likely to have never spent a moment of time anywhere near this river.

Over the past few months, the routine had been the same: Wake up, make breakfast, head out for the mornings work, cigarette break, back to work until last light, then dinner and back to bed in his flimsy tent on the ground at the base of a hill near the shore of the river.

Then sleep, and right back to *point A*.

Every day, he spent hour after hour hiking up and down the banks of the river, stopping here and there, dipping his pie pan into the water and sifting through layer after layer of silt, searching for signs of the lifeblood of the areas economy, raw unrefined gold. Since May, his pan showed him nothing other than his own reflection in the clear water floating over the empty dark brown silt as it passed through the nail holes and back into the river. Here today in June of 1848 nothing seems to have changed. Just a refection of his own unshaven, suntanned face starring back at him through the slowly disappearing water.

"Damn." Thomas grunted to himself before dipping the pan back into the water.

Again, nothing,

"God damn it!" He shouted as he heaved his pan at the ground, clearly fed up with the seemingly fruitless effort he had been putting himself through.

"Damn it!" He shouted again as he turned his back to the river, his voice echoing across the valley.

"Is there a problem here?" Called a voice from somewhere behind Thomas, "Because if there is a problem, I may have to ask you to leave."

"Ask me to leave?" Thomas asked, "Who's there?"

"Sir, I'm going to need you to calm down." The voice said.

"I am calm!" Thomas shouted as he pored over his surroundings trying to figure out where the voice was coming from.

"Calm people don't shout, sir," The voice replied, "now please, calm down. We can talk about this."

"Talk about what?" Thomas asked as he scratched his head under his hat.

"Are you going to calm down?" The voice asked, "Because if you aren't going to calm down, we aren't going to be able to have a pleasant conversation. You'll just get loud, I'll call security, and you'll be escorted out. It won't be fun. Believe me, it's in your best interests to just calm down and let me speak to you.. So are you going to calm down?"

"I… I guess so." Thomas barked.

"That doesn't sound calm."

"Listen friend," Thomas said, "I've been out here in the wild working for a couple of months now. It's hot, its tedious, and I have nothing to show for any of my work. I apologize if I'm coming across as hostile, but I honestly don't mean it. Its just that, as it turns out, voices coming out of thin air put me on edge. Who knew, right?"

"My voice isn't coming out of thin air." The voice said with a hint of bewilderment, "I'm right here."

"Where?"

"Right here!" The voice shouted.

"Are you invisible or something?" Thomas asked as his head darted around trying to figure this all out, "Are you some kind of ghost? An angel? Are you death himself coming to make a widow of my poor wife Clara?"

"Am I a ghost?" The voice asked, stunned, "Is that a real question?"

"Ghosts are invisible…"

"I'm not a ghost!"

"Then what are you?!"

"I'm James," He said, "I'm a man just like you."

"Then why can't I see you?"

"Well," James said, "The simple answer is that you just aren't looking hard enough."

"What does *that* mean?"

"It means that you aren't looking hard enough!" James said with frustration in his voice, "Because I am right fucking next to you!"

Thomas turned and looked to his left and finally found where James's voice was coming from, he was sitting at a desk right next to Thomas, the bottom of it situated in the very river Thomas had spent his entire morning panning in. He didn't recognize James, in fact, he seemed strange. His clothing was not befitting of a day out in the sun. He was dressed similar to the bankers that he remembered meeting up in San Francisco back when he purchased his plot of land. The jacket of his suit seemed thick, woolen, and capable of substantial heat retention. His trousers and waistcoat seemed like much of the same. His feet were understandably bare. No one wants runoff river water filling up their shoes and soaking through their socks.

His desk was as fabulous as it was massive. Its handsome dark wood was polished so completely that Thomas could easily make out his own reflection in its surface from a good two feet away. Its legs displayed a natural design featuring countless leaves and buds and flowers and vines so intricately constructed that Thomas thought they might be real.

"That there's a mighty fine desk you have," Thomas said, "It'd be a shame if it got all waterlogged from sitting in the river."

"No worries," James replied, "It's waterproof. Completely sealed. Nothing's getting in or out."

"The woodwork is lovely," Thomas said as he admired the carvings in the legs, "Where'd you get it done? Europe?"

"I did it all myself, actually." James answered, "Carved the whole thing out of a single piece of rosewood."

"Rosewood, huh?" Thomas asked, "A single piece you say?"

"Yessir!" James acknowledged him with a smile.

Thomas contemplated this for a moment before dropping everything in his hands and running full speed towards his campsite. James watched as Thomas fumbled through his belongings. He did his best to keep an eye on James as he continued to toss about through his old infantry knapsack from back in the days he spent in Texas fighting in the Mexican-American War. He dug and dug until he pulled out his trusty Colt Percussion .44 and pointed it at James. James smiled as he raised his hands up to assure Thomas that he meant no harm.

"What's this about?" James asked

"Where'd you find a piece of rosewood big enough to carve a desk that size?"

"I…" James stuttered, "I got it from the Yucatan…"

"What's a Yucatan?" Thomas asked, his hands shaking as he kept his gun trained on James.

"It's a state in Mexico." James clarified.

"I knew it!" Thomas shouted, "Your one of Santa Ana's spies, aren't you?!"

"Santa Ana?" Asked James.

"Yes!" Thomas barked back, "Antonio Lopez De Santa Ana! Commander of the Mexican forces! You're here spying for him! He want's my land, doesn't he?!"

"Are you talking about the war?"

"I watched men, good American men, die at the hands of his army and I will be God damned if I am going to allow him to send in one of his spies to take my land away from me!"

"The war ended, Thomas. Months ago."

"Quiet, Spy!" Thomas shouted as he fired a shot into James's skull.

Thomas looked in disbelief as he watched the bullet pass right through him.

"Mexican sorcery." Thomas said as he lowered his gun, "That's the only explanation."

"The *only* explanation?" James asked, "Are you sure about that?"

"That, or you're a ghost like I said before."

"Or," James smiled, "I was never really here to begin with."

Thomas dropped his gun when he came to the realization that he was standing alone at the edge of the river. The sun must be getting to him again. This isn't the first time he found himself shooting at ghosts while out on one of his panning expeditions and it surely wouldn't be his last.

Why are they always named James?

He should head home, Clara's probably worried.

Driving

Driving and I have a bit of a sorted history.

1999 was a year that saw the world edge closer and closer to a new millennium and the sense that it would bring about something new made its way across the country at a breakneck speed. Would the next thousand years be different than the last thousand? No one knew, and that was exciting. All we had to work with was the fiction that we were inundated with since some time in the early fifties. Many of those post world war science fiction tales held out hope that humanity might someday get their shit together and advance beyond all of this war and fighting nonsense that we had used to define ourselves for such a long time.

Back then, the year 2000 was something to look forward to. A specific, well rounded number. A time that wasn't so far off that it was inconceivable for those people to live and see it, yet far enough away that it could still represent an unreal age that will be filled with fantastic technologies and socially progressive mindsets that they could never comprehend.

At least they got the technological part right.

By 1999, communication technology had become a real site to see. Cellular technology was still in its awkward in between phase where we didn't have to hold giant space bricks against our face to make a phone call, but we had yet to fathom the idea of a phone representing 99% of human knowledge sitting snugly in our pockets. Looking back now, from the far off year of 2019, the communication technologies of the late 90's were laughably simplistic. We had to type 4-4-3-3-5-5-5-5-5-5-6-6-6 to text the word hello to our friends! Hell, if we were sending the message to a pager (Which were still things back then) we would type 43770 and we were fairly confident that the person we were saying it to could read it. I sure as shit could. The language of texting pagers in the late 90's was a language that only ever existed in that one very specific time period. Those of us who are now in our thirties are very likely some of the only people on the planet who could read it. 15177*7487*612824'?

Those socially progressive mindsets, however, were still a bit of a pipe dream. War and humanity seem to be a couple of concepts that go hand in hand. Since the end of World War 2 and the present day

---

1   Isn't that crazy?

there have been some two hundred and fifty major wars that have resulted in the deaths of over fifty million people. That was after the second world war which was the second time the world went to war with the hopes of snuffing out the very idea of war as a concept in and of itself. Nuts to that, I guess. Why do away with the idea of marginalizing entire parts of the human population and exerting power over one another when we can, you know, just keep doing all that?

In 1999, there were wars and conflicts taking place all over the world. Humanity hadn't even come close to finding new ways to just fucking get along with each other. I'm told that the geo-political implications of all the wars that are always going on at any given time or place throughout the world are necessary to the well being of society on a world scale and that I simply can't comprehend all of the in's and out's that need to exist for the world to work the way it does. To that I say, maybe the world *shouldn't* work the way it does. If the deaths of millions upon millions of human beings in places I have never heard of are necessary to the well being of the way society works, then maybe the way society works should change.

I am FAR from the first person to say this and I am certainly not going to be the last, but hey, it couldn't help to try and keep the idea of world peace alive, right? It's a concept that should be held by everyone, but unfortunately there are many people out there that don't want to hear it. So just keep spreading the word I guess. It really can't be that controversial, right?

So, right about now you might be asking yourself why I have gone off onto these tangents of technology and war and world peace in this paper that started out talking about my sorted history of driving.

Well, the reality of the situation is that I have issues with keeping on track, but I am going to go ahead and point out the fact that it all started with me discussing the year 1999. Not only was it the year that marked the culmination of the classic Y2K hysteria; 1999 was the year I turned sixteen. The legal age to drive an automobile in the state of California. 1999 is the year that my sorted history with driving cars started.

In the movies, when a kid turns sixteen, they wake up on their birthday excited about the fact that their driver's test is later in the day. Then some sort of wacky shenanigans take place that keep them from getting their license before the climax of the film that finds them finally getting to the DMV and taking their test and getting their license. Huzzah, everything goes good for movie boy.

I didn't get my license until I was eighteen.

But 1999, my sixteenth year of life, the first year I was able to legally drive a car, was indeed the year I first drove a car, albeit, not necessarily legally.

When I was sixteen, all of my friends started driving. As far as I know, they all got to experience those wacky movie scenarios, earning their right to drive a car by overcoming the scheming of whatever antagonist had made its way into their lives. I never got to experience one of those scenarios. No one showed up on my sixteenth birthday in need of a driver to help them out of an extravagant situation. I couldn't tell you what happened on my sixteenth birthday. As far as I can remember, it was just another nondescript day where nothing of note happened and then I got some cake. To be fair to me though, my memory is pretty much gone these days, so the details of most days are pretty much missing. Lost to the whims of brain plaques and spinal lesions.

1999 may not have been the year that I got my drivers license, but it was indeed the beginning of my sorted history with the automobile. It was the year that I first drove a car when I shouldn't have been driving. My friends with their licenses let me drive their cars on occasion, which looking back at now was an extremely stupid thing to do, but there's no way to take that back, so it is what it is. I drove my buddy's truck on several occasions, to head out and pick up pizza for the party where I was the only person who was either still sober or without the affections of the opposite sex to hold me back. Why pay for a delivery when you can send your unlicensed, uninsured friend to the parlor to pick it up? It happened several times and there were never any problems. Incredibly stupid, but all turned out okay, so there's no point in reprimanding myself now, right?

Not to get back into my prior habit of discussing world history randomly during my random story, but here I go doing exactly that.

2001 was a year that I will never forget. As far as I am concerned, no matter how far along this MS progresses, my memories of 2001 will never manage to go away. If they ever do, I will be far passed gone and would appreciate it if you would put a bullet through my brain, thanks. 2001, of course, is the year of good old 9/11. The year terrorists may or may not have flown commercial aircraft into multiple targets, destroying both the classic New York skyline and many American's ability to think rationally. Freedom fries! Don't let the terrorists win! Marginalize entire swaths of the population in exactly the way the terrorists you don't want to let win said you would! Patriotism indeed!

But none of that is what I am talking about here.

If I woke up tomorrow with no recollection of 9/11 and was promptly informed of it happening, I doubt I would bat an eye. If I woke up tomorrow with no recollection of the other major life event that happened to me in 2001 and were told about it later, I would be sent into a deep depression because I will know that my shit memory is finally starting to take its toll.

2001 is the year my daughter was born.

When she was born, my stupid ass finally realized that it was time to to get to driving.

And get to driving I did.

I got my license and started driving everywhere. Work, play, you name it, if me or my family needed to get there, I was right behind the wheel making it happen. I was happy to help. Significant other needs transportation to and from school? Done. Grandma needs a ride to her doctor's appointment? Done. Kid needs to go to school? Let's go, kid! I was happy to do it. All of it. I wouldn't necessarily say I loved driving. I enjoyed the time I got to spend with my loved ones as I got to help them along on their own paths. But the driving itself always took a back seat to the people I got to spend my time with. I loved them all.

My sister always used to joke that I drive like an old woman. Slow and steady. I would like to refute those claims, but the reality of it is that I can't. Like I said before, driving to me was never anything more than a way to get from one place to another. A leisurely activity that was meant to feel more like a nice warm hug than a zooming death trap speeding its way towards an ultimate demise in a spectacular wreck! I was just too easy going to drive aggressively man. I'm much more of a Wooderson than an O'Bannion. I'm more The Dude than Walter.

Movie references.

My crutch.

You're welcome.

I went through three cars before my initial MS diagnosis. A Ford Aerostar, a Ford Taurus, and a Ford Mustang. Apparently I'm a Ford man. The Aerostar was my favorite. A big dopey minivan. Like something your mom drove! I loved its big stupid boxy body[2]. I loved its sliding doors, its removable seats, the amount of room, I loved that van. I got it when it was already over ten years old and had reached that dreaded 100,000 mile mark. But it drove, and that was all I really needed. One night, while on my way to pick up my significant other from work, I was pulled over by several police officers. I had been pulled over before, no big deal, right? Well, the officer's drawn weapons felt differently. That mixed with the fact that my one year old

---

2   Like your mom again, right?

was in sleeping in her baby carrier in the back seat made the ordeal all the more terrifying. As it turns out, they were looking for someone who had very recently robbed a store or something and my shitty van matched their vehicle description. As shitty as that was, all I could think of after the fact was how silly it was that they robbed someone in such an easily identifiable vehicle. Usually cars that are older than ten years old stand out on the road, especially when they are the kinds of vehicles that look like giant boxes lumbering on by. Just a random aside, never mind any of that…

My first big MS relapse put me in the hospital for a month. It fundamentally changed the way my body works. Most importantly to the topic at hand, how my body acts when it is in motion.

Basically, any speed faster than my natural walking pace sends my brain a-swimming. I start to feel like I am floating underwater, unable to tell which way is up. It's extremely disabling. Imagine feeling buzzed at all times, then when you start to move you feel flat out drunk.

Yea. We can't have that behind the wheel of a massive steel death machine. So yea, no more driving for me.

Now, I am one of those bus riding regulars that your parents told you about. I am the handicapped gimp that rides on the train and hates how quick some people are to feel bad and give up their seat. It's appreciated, no doubt, but it's also a somewhat painful reminder that I am not the person that I used to be. As much as I hate to admit it, I am now defined by my illness.

It is what it is.

And it's my sorted history with driving that is primarily to blame, right?

Suburban Morons

The bored mind of a suburban youth left to its own devices may one day prove to be one of the most dangerous natural phenomenon known to human kind.

This isn't just the cantankerous contention of some thirty something curmudgeon, mind you. This is something that I know from experience.

In my youth, I myself was an average suburban kid. Conventional to the core. A mundane specimen of the human race with nothing real to offer society, always searching in vain for a purpose. An inherent need to find some sort of meaning to cut through all the banal frivolity that encapsulated every waking moment of my life.

They say that by the time you are in your thirties, you should no longer be friends with the people you knew in high school. The idea being that as you mature, you leave those people behind. You realize that you no longer have anything in common with them and you were only actually friends out of convenience. The size of the world that you lived in was so small that there was a finite amount of people around for you to find solace in. Now that you are a big powerful adult, you get to pick and choose your friends! If you meet someone you think you might get along with, just hand them your business card and BAM! New friend!

I think that the people who feel this way just didn't make the right kinds of friends in their youth. Sure, there are plenty of people that I knew as a kid whom I haven't spoken a word to in years. People who I would have called my best friends back then are now pretty much strangers. With the advent of social media, I am still able to see how they're doing, and I am happy to see that they are living their best lives, but I wouldn't call them friends anymore. I don't care how hard Facebook tries to push that idea. They are the people that I used to know.

Making friends in adulthood as a concept is complete bullshit. You have acquaintances that you know from work and the parents of your kids friends. Just like in your youth, as an adult you are forced into friendships purely out of convenience.

That isn't to say I never found lasting friendships.

I am thirty six years old and I can confidently say that I have two people in my life that I would consider to be friends. I am closer to them than anyone I have ever known throughout my entire life and they are both people that I met in high school. With one of them, the argument could be made that the friendship has only lasted out of convenience. That really isn't something I could argue, but that's a different story for a different day. *(2022 Update: It DID last out of convenience and I should rethink the friendship aspect!)*

Today we are discussing the idiocy of suburban youth, and nothing on this planet could exemplify this concept better than the foundations of my friendship with the man whom to this day I still consider my best friend.

He knows who he is. You don't need to know his name.

But for brevity's sake, let's just call him Erik.

I first met Erik in 1998. Sophomore year of high school. He had noticed some stupid game that I would regularly play with another student that we both knew by the name of BJ. The game was simple: BJ would draw an elaborate picture that usually consisted of both a monster, and a representation of a hero that I would control. He would draw up some nonsense stats and ask me what I wanted to do in order to defeat the monster. I would come up with something bizarre and BJ would decide how many hit points would be taken away from the monster. A stupid twist on the classic Dungeons & Dragons. It was what we would have called retarded, because this was the 90s and we could still call things retarded back then.

So Erik had seen us playing this game and he wanted to know how it worked, he wanted to understand the ins and outs of what made it tick, and most of all he wanted in on the fun. For a time, I refused to tell him how the game worked. I mean, there weren't any rules really, it worked based entirely on the whims of BJ's design, but that wasn't what he wanted to hear. He pestered me for days. The days turned into months and the months turned into years until now, nearly twenty years later, he is still pestering me on a daily basis. I honestly don't know how I would cope if it ever stopped.

After explaining the game, Erik was eventually allowed to join in on the fun and the strangest, most bizarre adventure of my life began.

Several weeks into our dumb, entirely nonsensical friendship, Erik invited me over to his house. He gave me directions to get there: Walk down Gressel Street like you are going to the Swim Club, then turn right on Meadowbrook Avenue and walk down to the end where I would find a blue house with his mother's car parked in the driveway. I followed his directions to a T, and for the life of me I couldn't find his house. I searched up and down that street (well...) for a good half an hour before finally realizing that the his directions were wrong. I needed to turn left on Meadowbrook. Once I figured that out, finding his house was a breeze. To this day, Erik maintains that he gave me the proper directions, but I assure you that he didn't and after knowing him for as many years as I have, I am fairly certain that he gave me the wrong directions on purpose.

One time, I spent the night at his house.

Early in the night, he showed me a feature in a copy of Penthouse that he had where the magazine gave a recipe for the fake cum that they use in their videos. One of the selling points of it was that it even TASTED like cum! Weird, sure, but like I had said before, we were suburban morons searching for reason in an unreasonable world. We found our reason that night when we mixed up a large batch of fake cum, loaded it into a super-soaker, and sprayed it all over the neighborhood. On peoples doors, on parked cars, everywhere. People were going to come out of their houses in the morning and see the cum all over their cars and just wonder where it all came from!

We had the perfect image in our minds:

"What?!" the fictional elderly man would scream, "Where did all of this CUUUUUM come from?!"

We laughed and laughed and laughed at the idea of it all.

In reality, I doubt anyone even noticed that anything had happened. At the very least, they would have seen strange smudges on their windshields and cleaned them off, completely oblivious to the fact that two young boys had sprayed their cum all over their windshield.

But that didn't matter to us.

All we needed was a brilliant idea, and with that one little spark, we would keep ourselves entertained.

We certainly managed to keep ourselves entertained.

Emotional baggage mixed with a general malaise and a contempt for polite society was what we had in common. We were an exemplification of the blasé generation X mindset that had come before us living within a millennial society that had yet to become aware that it was millennial. The year 2000 was coming for us at a breakneck pace and we couldn't care less. The idea of a connected society coming together to share in the vastness of human knowledge meant nothing to us. We were much more concerned with seeing what happens when we would dial 1-800-DANCREEDEN into the school's payphone.

It called Radio City Music Hall.

I tried to hire the Rockettes for my non existent nephew's third birthday party.

It didn't come to fruition.

I stated before that we were prime examples of what happens when suburban youths get bored and scratch their boredom itch in the most asinine ways, but in reality, all we were doing was having a good time. We found our own fun, and despite the fact that we thought we were effecting everyone around us in a negative way, we weren't actually hurting anyone.

We were us.

Ourselves, through and through.

No one else can say that.

The Simpler Future of the Past

Somewhere, far out in the dark silent vastness of the universe there's bound to exist every idea and concept that your inferior primate brain can comprehend. Your deepest fears and greatest desires hiding out where you can never go. Not for lack of desire, of course. Perhaps one day technology will make it all possible, traveling through the vastness of the universe in an attempt to make your dreams come true.

But when your scope of reality gets bigger, wouldn't your hopes and dreams follow suit? Why keep your hopes and dreams so simple when you have ample ability to just think bigger? When I was a kid, the idea of having all of the world's knowledge readily available in my pocket seemed like some kind of far off fantasy. It was all a bunch of sci-fi hooey. It was the kind of technology I would see on Star Trek every week. Picard would ask the ships computer a question and it would answer him. I can do the same thing with my cell phone now. No, I can't travel through the cosmos under warp power, I don't have a curious android for a friend, and none of my blind friends are wearing spiffy sci-fi visors that give them sight, but what we *do* have has been just as revolutionary. Everyday we're getting closer and closer to those sweet Geordie LaForge glasses.

My point here, of course, is that in my lifetime I've been privy to a technological revolution that's been integrated into everyday life so seamlessly that it has been almost completely invisible. The home computer was initially advertised to us as just another home appliance, something that can make our everyday lives just a little bit easier; a tool to help us accomplish everyday tasks in a simpler way. It would help students with their schoolwork in much the same way a stand mixer helps a chef with their cook work. What they didn't tell us was the potential that was hiding inside of that silly little box that was now sitting in all of our homes. In no time, they all had crazy noises bellowing out from internal modems that managed to connect us to the brand new wild west that was the internet of the 1990's. Sure, it was something that nerds had been doing for quite some time, but the closest a majority of the greater public had come to understand of the internet came from having seen the 1983 film Wargames. The one where Matthew Broderick uses a rotary phone to connect to the pentagon. Sure, it may have been somewhat accurate, but it was still more of the aforementioned sci-fi hooey to damn near everyone who saw the movie.

The old internet certainly was a thing to behold. The old internet that I remember, of course. Everyone with the slightest bit of know how had a website dedicated to Star Wars, or The X-Files, or pretty much anything your little heart desired. Sure, we still have those kinds of websites today, but back then, they were simple and to the point. They were crudely slapped together, they looked terrible, and the information was questionable, but that was how we liked it. Chat rooms and message boards were there for us to go discuss all of the information and argue about the accuracy therein. And the best part of all this was the lack of advertising. Holy shit, you can't go online anymore without being inundated with targeted advertisements designed specifically to make you feel paranoid. My phone is sitting next to me right now and there is a slight concern in the back of my head that it is listening to me, hearing the clacking of my keyboard and generating a series of targeted advertisements for Star Trek, Wargames, and any number of subjects that it deciphered from the order of the specific keys I am currently hitting.

The old internet soon turned into the new internet. The previously mentioned advertisements took the place of the nuance that was hiding under the surface and it has never been the same. I once dreamed of the ability to play video games with people from all over the world, but now that I have experienced exactly what it's like to have a twelve year old claim to be balls deep in my mother, I no longer care for it. I can go experience entire virtual worlds populated by nothing other than actual flesh and blood human beings who are also experiencing the same thing in real time, and all it's able to accomplish is to inform me that I am living in a real world that is populated by the very same disgusting degenerates that are living on the internet.
The world used to be fun, now it isn't.
I blame 9/11.
I always do. We let the terrorists win.

Room

Four walls, a ceiling, and a floor.

No windows, no doors, no connection to what's outside.

Just four walls, a ceiling, and a floor.

That, of course, is what my life has deteriorated to over the passed few years. Four walls, a ceiling, and a floor. I know I said no windows and no doors, but that isn't entirely true. The windows exist, as do the doors, but they haven't been used for their intended purposes for so long that they're better off left forgotten. Some time ago, the glass windows were covered with enough newspaper and tin foil that any light they manage to let in was stopped in its tracks by the thick set of curtains hanging in front of them. I forget what's on the other side. I assume it's the outside, but I can't be sure. The only way to know would be to peel away the layers of newspaper and foil and take a look, but that's out of the question.

Perhaps it's more of the inside; a mirror looking back at me to remind me that I'm stuck here and there is very little I can do to change it.

The doors might as well just be considered a part of the wall at this point. They've sat there closed, for so long now that it would surprise me if they're even still capable of being opened, the hinges rusted shut from years of disuse.

I can't seem to recall when I lost count of the days. I can remember when I was at five, feeling as if I had just spent a year in total solitude, but I cant seem to remember when it actually did become a year. It's been a blur for ages now. The years seem to be flying by these days, but I can't help but question whether that is actually the case or not. I haven't seen the sun in so long that I can't be sure that it's still there. For all I know, the darkness of my closed off room extends far beyond the borders of my reality, darkening the world that I used to know and helping it to become another piece of the puzzle I find myself trapped in.

I can recall faces. People from my past who I vaguely still remember flashing through my memories and refusing to leave. An eye here, a tuft of hair there; all pieces to a puzzle who's completion is no longer relevant. I remember names as well. Simple words meant to describe the faces that only come in flashes. Meaningless words that serve no other purpose than to remind me that I am completely and utterly alone.

Time still seems to exist here. Regardless of whether or not I choose to keep track of it, the rush of time passing me by never seems to leave me be. The past and present blend together so completely that I have trouble telling the two apart sometimes. Is it now? Is it then? Is then now, or will now never pass? I know that now is always now, but once I recognize it as now, the now has passed and becomes then. Now I'm in a new now, but that now is already a new then. It passes so fast that I might as well consider them one in the same. The time it takes for thoughts to form within my head renders the present completely inconsequential. I can only recognize the world in the past tense and I hold no bearing over the presence of the present.
The future is my only certainty. It stays out in front of me, reminding me that there is nothing there, nothing certain other than the cold embrace of death.

But even that is an uncertainty here. I have been sitting in this room for so long that I have no recollection of how I got here. Am I even really here? The makeup of here is engulfed entirely in darkness, its descriptions the result of an ever failing memory and a questionable state of mind, so how can I even know that here is what I think it is?

Let's think on this for a moment. If here is what I assume it to be, what I described it as earlier, then how did I get here? Was it through choices I made throughout my life that brought me to this point where I am alone, sitting in complete darkness, ruminating on the reality of my questionable surroundings very existence? Or is the here in question the choice itself? Am I here because I choose to be here? Is here only here because I'm telling myself that it is? Are these questions pertinent to what's going on around me? Is anything going on around me? Does any of this matter?

All I know is that I'm stuck, whether it is here or elsewhere, I am stuck and I'm not sure how to get out. All I know is the void of darkness that surrounds me.

Darkness is a strange concept when you think about it. Often times it is compared to the sight of the blind. If you find yourself stuck behind a veil of absolute darkness, it is as good as not being able to see at all. The thing is, you can still see. You can see the darkness, which is something a blind man can't see. Their world isn't black. They don't see darkness, they simply don't see. The world around them exists in the same way it exist for one with sight; the only real difference being in the way its comprehended.

The world to the eyes of the sighted could be described by the many varying colors that it projects out from itself, or by the way the shapes look in comparison to other shapes around them. A blind man may comprehend these very same shapes in an entirely different way. He might describe to you how it sounds when his voice bounces off of it or how it feels when he rubs his hand against it. These descriptions may vary greatly in all the subtle nuance that is put into them, but at the end of the day, they are all accurate. They all describe the same thing as best as the describer is able to describe them and they all work out in different ways.

My room, or whatever you want to call it, is one that I can only describe to you as dark. It has been years since I have ventured forward from this spot and attempted to feel out how exactly this place is put together. My memory of the past where I could still remember the room as it were consists mainly of the idea of four walls, a ceiling, and a floor. I vaguely remember windows and doors, so I include them in my description, but I'm still not sure if I should trust my memory.

I'm not even sure I remember having arms or legs or a body. I don't recall ever being able to feel them or move them or even know what they were all about. If I put in some effort, perhaps I can move forward, find one of those windows, throw open its curtains and tear down its coverings and wash myself in the light of the outside world.

But that all seems so hard.

I would rather exist here, in a world of darkness of my own creation, where the past is a blur, the present is past, and the future bears only the bitter fruit of incomplete puzzles and broken realizations.

This is where I belong.

In a darkness that I refuse to overcome.

Emptiness is all I deserve.

Grandma

The room was brightly lit, just the way she liked it. The white walls reflecting the morning sun with a brilliance that could only be considered an overstatement when you consider that they were simply white painted walls in a suburban bedroom. She lay in her bed, the blankets covering her from toe to elbow, exposing to the world her face, a face that wore a life well lived with hanging skin and wrinkles that screamed out her advanced years to anyone who might look in her direction. The amount of history and knowledge that she had lived through was evident to anyone who might take a moment to listen to her when she spoke.   Unfortunately, those who might listen are few and far between these days and the amount of time she had, both for conscious thought and for life itself, were winnowing down day by day.

Morning was her favorite time of day. Not just for the bowl of cold cereal and the glass of coffee that I would bring her, but because in the morning, her facilities were all intact. After a night of lapsed reasoning, hallucinations, and flat out dementia, the mornings meant she got to be a person again. She got to experience the world as it existed and not as a series of neurological misfires telling her that some of her worst fears were coming true. She wasn't fully aware of this, of course, that's the nature of dementia, you're never completely aware of what's happening. Whether or not she had any sort of recall to these episodes after they occurred was a mystery to me. She never spoke of them after the fact and I never actually sat down to discuss them with her. I didn't want her to feel afraid.

"Good morning, Grandma." I said as I walked in through her bedroom door, bringing her morning coffee

"Oh!" Grandma exclaimed, startled by my apparently sudden appearance, "You scared me!"

"I'm sorry," I replied, "I just wanted to bring you your coffee."

"Oh its fine dear," She said as she adjusted herself in her bed in order to sit more upright, "Please, set in on my night stand."

As I crossed the room with her coffee, my nose began to twitch as it started to pick up on the fetid odor that had permeated the room throughout the night hours. Getting out of her bed and using the bathroom at night had become increasingly more and more difficult for her over the past few years and in that time it had become my responsibility to clean out the plastic commode that she was forced to use when nature called out to her.

I set the coffee down on her night stand and she reached out for my hand, grasping it tightly and smiling to me as if to thank me without having to actually say the words. I squeezed her grip back to her and returned her smile, letting her know that it wasn't a problem. There are no limits to what one might do in the name of family, be it delivering a simple cup of coffee in the morning or washing out a bucket full of piss and shit, nothing's off the table for the ones we love.

"I'll just take this." I said as I picked up the commode and began to carry it out of the room. "Oh," I turned and looked back before exiting the room, "Do you want some cereal?"

"I'd love some." She replied.

"Raisin Bran okay?" I asked, trying my damnedest to ignore the odor rising up from below me.

"That's perfect." She answered with a smile.

I carried the commode down the hallway and out to the garage where I set it down next to the large plastic utility sink that rested in between the washer and the dryer. Not wanting to allow the stench of its contents to seep out too far, I quickly got to work cleaning it out. A utility sink such as this isn't meant for the disposal of solid waste. Its undersized drain and narrow piping set was used mainly as a berth for the draining of used water from inside of the washing machine. The machine would drain its water, after completing its wash cycle into the sink and send the water off through the pipes to wherever they might lead.   Normally, solid waste would gather up inside these narrow pipes and cause a backup, something not unheard of in modern day plumbing circles, but still something that is best avoided. Solid waste was certainly a no-no for this sink and I was well aware of this. Human waste is normally solid, we all know this, but asking a ninety year old woman to properly digest her solid intake and dispose of it through her bowels in a solid form is next to impossible. The bucket on this commode was filled with human waste, but it was far from solid human waste. Washing it down the garage sink wouldn't be a problem at all. It would be gross; disgusting even, but like I said before, there are no limits to what we are willing to do for those we love.

With a handkerchief wrapped around my face, I removed the waste bucket from the commode and got to work cleaning it out. Like I said before, it was gross. I did as one might expect; I poured the contents of the bucket down the sink, washed it all out with soap and hot water, and only gagged four times as opposed to the usual six.

On my way to return the commode to my grandmother's room I stopped off at the bathroom and grabbed a bottle of aerosol air freshener. I brought it to the room and sprayed it in order to get rid of the stench. At the very least it would cover it up and my grandmother wouldn't have to sit in the smell.

"Thank you, dear." She said as I sprayed the room, "You know, I really appreciate you doing all this for me."

"It's my pleasure, Grandma."

*   *   *   *   *

When I brought her cereal to my grandmother's room, I found her sipping at her coffee while intently reading the newspaper. I'm not sure what the story she had been reading was all about, nor am I even sure that she fully understood what she was reading, but as I set her cereal down on her night stand I couldn't help but notice the agitated look on her face as her eyes scanned the page.

"I can't believe what kind of money they want for a car these days." She said, "thirty seven thousand dollars?"

"Well," I said, "Are you looking at a luxury car? They tend to be over priced these days."

"It's a," She began before looking for the name of the car on the page, "Lexus. A Lexus RX 350. It looks like it's some kind of a van. Almost forty thousand dollars for a van, can you believe it?"

"I can," I said as I looked over her shoulder at what she was looking at. "People pay a lot of money for status symbols these days. Besides, that isn't a van; it's a sport utility vehicle. Very en vogue."

"SUV, Van, whatever, they're all the same to me." She quickly replied.

"Yea, except you can fit more than five people into a van!" I laughed

She smiled as she continued to look at the paper.

"What is a Lexus anyway?" She asked.

"I think it's the luxury branch of Toyota." I answered.

"Toyota?" She shot back, "The Japanese company?"

"Yep."

"They built the trucks that carried the troops that tried and failed to kill your grandfather in World War 2 and now, good, hard working Americans are paying fifty thousand dollars to look like fancy lads driving around in one of their cars. It's a shame."

"I... I mean, it's been sixty three years... We live in a different..."

I stammered, dumbfounded, for a time as she watched stone faced. After a bit, I saw the look on her face crack and a smile began to stretch across it. In time, her smile turned into a laugh. A fun laugh, one that showed that even in her advanced years and depleting physical state, she was still full of life and capable of showing it.

"I'm kidding!" She barked out, putting an end to my mindless stammering, "I drove a Honda back in the eighties, and trust me, their hands aren't clean either!"

I pondered this for a moment before allowing myself to laugh. I was always happy to hear from my grandmother when she was of a sound mind, when she was able to comprehend the world around her and have fun with it. It was getting to the point where I was starting to miss that woman, but times like this came and went at a somewhat regular pace and I was grateful for them.

*   *   *   *   *

I liked to keep my room dark at night, lit only by the light of the television that I was watching as I laid down to rest at the end of the day. I tended to stay awake later than the other people who lived in the house, so I tried to keep it quiet by keeping the volume on my television low. Not too low as to hinder my ability to hear what was happening on it, but still low enough to keep me able to hear what was going on beyond my closed bedroom door.

As I laid there watching the news, or Nick at Nite, or some other banal pointless nonsense, I faintly heard from the other side of my door the sound of the front door of the house opening and a muffled voice.

I knew exactly what was happening, this was far from the first time my grandmother had experienced an episode such as this. She had an episode at least once a week, but they were becoming more and more frequent at this point. I knew how to deal with them calmly and rationally, but the increased frequency was making it harder and harder every time. Seeing someone you love losing their mind is nerve wracking and having to see it happen on and off with increased frequency was enough to drive someone mad.

"Grandma," I said, rushing down the hallway, "What's wrong?"

She had been standing at the front door of the house, shouting out the door at someone who wasn't there. She looked around for a bit as if completely unaware of her surroundings before looking at me and addressing me as if I were my father.

"Dan, it's your sister," She said matter-of-factly, "I told her on the phone not to come here, but she did anyway."

"Grandma, no one's here." I said as I put my hand on her shoulder and guided her away from the door.

"It's your sister. She said she was going to come here and take me away." She said

"Grandma, she isn't here." I said in a calm voice, "Let's get you back to bed, okay, everything is going to be alright."

I closed the door behind me as I began to lead her back to her room. She came along with me without question, slowly taking each step before stopping entirely and gasping audibly.

"No," she shouted, "I don't want to go."

"Grandma, it's okay, it's just me." I assured her, hoping to placate her fear.

"I won't go." She said again.

"Grandma, she isn't here." I tried to reason, "No one is trying to take you away."

"No, not your sister," She said, pointing into the darkness in front of herself, "Him."

"Grandma, there's no one there." I said, knowing my voice of reason was coming in vain.

"He," She squeezed out, clearly holding back tears, "He says he wants to take me away. He wants to take me away from here."

The thought of seeing someone who no one else can see is terrifying. Especially if that person is telling you they want to take you away somewhere. I can't imagine the kind of fear that was going through her mind at that moment. Who was the person she was seeing? Where did he want to take her? She was nearing the end of her life and she was fully aware of it. It is reasonable to assume that this man she was seeing was some sort of subconscious apparition that her mind conjured up as a grim reminder that the end was coming to take her into that unknown beyond. Maybe it was a coping mechanism that the mind creates as it becomes more and more aware that its death is coming soon. The thought is terrifying and I can't imagine the kind of fear it might bring about, especially considering the real people around you are assuring you that it isn't really there.

It's there.

It's always there, right behind you, waiting for your mind to be ready to comprehend it.

I helped my grandmother back into her room, assuring her everything would be okay the whole way, and helped her back into her bed. I kept my door open that night, waiting in my room for her to fall asleep. I laid there; awake, unable to think of anything other than the idea that she saw death there, right in front of her. Whether it was actually there or not is beyond the point. In her head, in that moment, whatever it was that she saw was there and it was begging her to come with it.

One day it will come to me and ask me to come with it.

Every day I think about that, every single day.

Some days it leaves me stiff and other days it is fleeting, but it is always there. Right behind me. Waiting for my mind to be truly ready to comprehend it.

Human Selfishness
is
Human Kindness

The end of the world is a lot more subjective than people tend to think. Fire and brimstone raining down from the heavens, the earth opening up to swallow everything above it and dragging it all down into hell. Angels and demons battling in the streets, supposedly in a struggle for the control of our souls. One side fighting to usher us into paradise while the other strives for the honor of raping our butts in an eternal furnace filled with pain and torment.

That's all nonsense. A fairy tale forced onto us by a societal structure that's existed for longer than society itself. Primitive man needed the threat of punishment to be constantly looming at the periphery of his thoughts in order to act in a way that was less harmful to himself and to those around him.

These days, the idea of the looming threat of eternal torment is laughable. We don't need to be constantly told to do the right thing any more. We've evolved in such a way that those kinds of supernatural threats are no longer relevant. We no longer need to be threatened to keep ourselves in line. Treating everyone properly is a reward all on its own.

Only that's all nonsense too.

People are selfish. Stupid and selfish. I don't care how intelligent or altruistic you think you are, at the end of the day if you had to choose between yourself and a stranger, regardless of the circumstances, you're going to choose yourself. Even when you think you're choosing the stranger, you're actually choosing yourself. You're helping others for your own stupid reasons. For your own good. You can lie to yourself and to the world all you want about what a magnanimous, charitable, loving, caring person you are, but the reality is and will always be that you are doing it for you.

You might be doing it for attention, "Look at me! I'm sooooooooo awesome for feeding this homeless man!".

You might be doing it to atone, "I may be horrible to everyone close to me, but at least I give back in order to make up for it!".

You might be doing it because somewhere deep down in those places in your mind that you work your hardest to avoid, you know that you hate yourself. You recognize the evolutionary path that you took that led you to the point that you are at now and you can see what a selfish, ugly, hateful person you are and you hate yourself for it.

Of course that all might just be me. I might just be projecting for the sake of projecting.

I might be attributing all of my own personal vices onto all of human kind in order to make myself feel better about the piece of shit person that I might actually be.

Maybe I should go make up for that.

I hear the children's hospital in Oakland accepts volunteers.

A volunteer army of well wishers fighting against their own ill will and shifty morals in a personal struggle to feel better about themselves.

But at the end of the day, helping out your fellow man in order to feel better about yourself is still helping your fellow man. Just because you post pictures of yourself working with disabled kids to your Instagram wall, bathing yourself in likes and cumming all over the fact that people think you're a decent human being doesn't change the fact that you very likely made someone else's day just a little bit better. It really is something to be commended.

Human selfishness is human kindness.

"But Dan," You might say, "What does any of this have to do with that comment you made at the top of the page about the end of the world?"

Well, I'll tell you.

When people think about the end of the world, they tend to think about it literally. All that fire and brimstone, heaven and hell nonsense that I discussed up there is a very real idea to a lot of people. You plug religion into anything and a lot of people start to take it seriously. That's fine, people can have their religion. If it's something that they need, more power to them.

Sometimes, when people think about the end of the world, they look at it more scientifically. A meteor slamming into the planet and snuffing out life as we know it. The sun suddenly exploding in a bright flash, burning away all life on earth and every remnant of any life that had ever existed here, all gone in an instant.

These are examples of the world ending in an objectively indisputable way. Life was there, now it isn't. It would be inarguable and it would be true to everyone alive to experience it. The literal end of the world is an objective concept.

When I say that the end of the world is more subjective, I am speaking more metaphorically.

There are certain things that could happen to me that would essentially snuff my world from existence and I am sure that if you think hard on it, the same could be said of something in your own life.

For example, my daughter is my world. She is my reason for waking up in the morning and the basis for everything good in my life.

If I ever lost her, my world would be gone.

All of the light would be extinguished from my existence.

That would be the end of the world.

For me.

It's an extremely self centered reality. Each and every one of us lives in our own little world where the ins and outs of how we live our lives go on unaffected by a significant portion of all the little worlds beyond our own. Everyone lives out their own personal experience completely separate from everyone else, ignorant to the whims of the world at large, and we all tend to focus primarily on our own well being and that of our own circle. There's nothing wrong with that either. Its what gives us purpose, a reason to keep going.

My world ending might have zero effect on you, and along with 99.99% of human kind, your life would go on without you ever batting an eye or even taking notice. You would remain blissfully unaware that there is now at least one person out there roaming the world without any reason to be doing so. A person without reason could be a very dangerous thing.

A cynical, misanthropic existence where your feelings and thoughts and ideals are meaningless. It's something that's true of a lot of people. Like I said before, people are selfish.

Stupid and selfish.

The Secret to a Long Life

The smell of his grandfather's hospice never sat well with Jeff. The smell of piss, vinegar, ointment, and bleach tended to linger in his nostrils for hours after he had left the building making it quite the ordeal to simply stop and smell the flowers. Jeff's grandfather's room was particularly smelly. At least that's how Jeff saw it. Perhaps it was because seeing his grandfather in there seemed wrong to him. Jeff had always seen his grandfather as a strong man, one who was capable of doing anything. Perhaps seeing him in this weakened state, laying helpless in this foul smelling room, forced Jeff's brain to assume that the smell was worse than it really was.

Perhaps it just smelled terrible in there.

Jeff's grandfather Ennis was born back in the year 1918. Just in time to fight for survival during the Spanish Flu epidemic as an infant, then go on to enjoy the Great Depression as a teen. And trust me, he was more than willing to tell Jeff all about it, whether he asked him to or not. He liked to tell Jeff all about how he was older than vacuum cleaners, windshield wipers, and the washing machine, depending on what Jeff had been complaining about at any given moment.

"Ugh, the washer didn't get the stain out of my t-shirt!" Jeff *would complain, assuming he was out of Ennis' earshot.*

"You know back in MY day," Ennis *would respond to Jeff's* dismay, *"washing machines weren't even a thing!"*

They were, of course. The washing machine was almost as old as the United States themselves, having been invented in 1797. These old colonial washing machines were still much more labor intensive than Jeff would be used to, which MIGHT have lent credence to Ennis' point had the electric washing machine not been invented in 1908, a full decade before Ennis was born. The same could be said for most of the points Ennis made.

Who knows when the washing machine was invented?

Ennis knew.

Ennis knew a lot of oddball facts.

The most important of which being that no one questions the nonsensical ramblings of an old man.

"Hey, grandpa." Jeff said as he entered the room.

Ennis just laid there.

"Hey grandpa?" Jeff said again, slightly louder this time, "Are you awake?"

"I don't have time to sleep, kid." Ennis answered, slowly opening his eyes.

"You don't have time to sleep?" Jeff responded, his voice oozing with incredulity, "What's keeping you so busy?"

Ennis raised his head and looked directly into Jeff's eyes.

"I am living in hospice, Jeffrey."

"Grandpa, I didn't mean to..."

"If I go to sleep," Ennis interrupted, "there isn't any guarantee that I'm going to wake up."

"Grandpa, don't talk like that." Jeff said, "I'm sure you have plenty of..."

"Plenty of what?" Ennis interrupted again, "Time? Jeffrey, I am one hundred years old. A century. I have seen a lot in my time."

"Time is relative," Jeff responded, not quite sure where he was going with this, "A hundred years to someone like me seems like a crazy unattainable amount of time, but to you, it's a reality!"

Ennis smirked to himself before he responded.

"Jeffrey, son," Ennis started as the smirk was slowly swept off from his face, "A hundred years IS a crazy amount of time. Yes, it is a reality to me. A reality that I am painfully aware of. I remember every moment of my life. Every breath is accounted for up here," Ennis tapped himself on the forehead, "Every word I ever spoke, every person I ever met, everything."

"Everything?" Jeff asked

"Everything." Ennis replied, "Test it. Name a date."

Jeff ponders this for a moment.

"Okay... August 6th, 1945." Jeff proposed.

"Really?" Ennis asked, skeptically.

"What?"

"August 6th, 1945..."

"Yea, what about it?"

"That's the day we dropped the atomic bomb on Hiroshima."

"Is it?"

"Yes! Don't they teach that in schools anymore?!"

"I'm sure they did... I just don't necessarily remember the date..."

Ennis stared at Jeff for a moment before shaking his head in a glaring and obvious show of disappointment in his bloodline.

"Well," Jeff broke the moment of silence, "You asked for a date. Go ahead, wow me!"

"Jeffrey, you gave me the date we dropped the first atomic bomb."

"Yea, you told me."

"That's like me asking you to tell me what you did on September 11th 2001. Of course you remember, that date's going to stick out to you a bit. It wouldn't be as mind blowing."

"Oh." Jeff said, "I guess that makes sense."

"So go ahead and give me another date."

"Okay... How about February 23, 1954?"

"Now, that's much better."

Ennis tilted his head up in a ponderous fashion, contemplating his actions on a day sixty four years earlier. A day that was widely known in certain communities as being the day that the first ever polio vaccines were administered. Ennis knew this, but he kept quiet. It wasn't important.

"Let's see, I ate fried eggs for breakfast and lunch, I met a nice young woman named Marcy at the Department of Motor Vehicles and I had a nice roast pork butt for dinner. I took somewhere around 24,058 breaths, I was awake for about eight hundred ninety five minutes, and I used the bathroom twelve times. I was drinking a lot of water that week."

None of this was true, of course, but Ennis knew Jeff wouldn't question it.

"That's..." Jeff said, somewhat taken a back, "Amazing."

"I know, right?"

Jeff sat, staring at his grandfather with a look of childlike wonder plastered across his face. He had always looked at his grandfather with that same sense of wonder, but this time it was different. Seeing a century's old man laying helpless in a hospice bed being able to recall his youth with clarity was something different. It was endearing. Something to be looked at with respect.

"How do you do it, grandfather?" Jeff queried.

"Do what?"

"How can you remember everything like that?"

"Why, the same way I have managed to live for so long."

"And how did you manage that?" Jeff asked

"Every day, since the day I turned ten," Ennis answered as Jeff leaned in closer to hear him better, "every single day, I searched for hours, trying to find the perfect rock. I couldn't really tell you what made each rock perfect, but when you find them, you know. I would take these perfect rocks home with me where I would spend the next hour or so inserting these perfect rocks into my anus."

"Into your anus?"

"Life has a price, my boy, it is up to you to decide if it's one you're willing to pay. Having a colon full of rocks tends to make a man *feel* more, *KNOW* more. Those rocks served as a constant reminder that life is... Fleeting. Life is too short to just let it pass by without taking stock of what you have and what you do. It made for a tough life, of course, but like I said, life has a price, and sometimes that price is a little hard to swallow. Other times, that price needs a little lube to help it along. I was willing to pay that price, every single day for ninety years, and I'll be damned if I fall asleep in hospice and never wake up. I came into this world screaming my guts out and I am dead set on going out the same way! Life is good, Jeffrey! Hold onto it for as long as you can. Do whatever you can to make it last!"

The nurses rushed into Ennis' room at the sound of his screams and Jeff looked on as his grandfather left the world in the way he had just promised to do so, screaming like a crazy person with a colon filled with shiny polished rocks.

Did Ennis actually shove rocks into his asshole on a daily basis in order to achieve an extended lifespan and a prolific sense of memory? Jeff may never know. We, however, know the truth. Ennis never stuck any rocks in his asshole. Not once. He just thought the story was a funny one to tell on his way out of this world and if it convinces Jeff to attempt to shove rocks into his own asshole, then it will make it a life well spent.

A life worth living.

RIP, Ennis
1918-2018
You will be missed.

Staring
(Thoughts from the Hospital, 2013)

I sit on my bed, trying my damnedest to watch the cars in the distance drive passed on the freeway. Blurry little globs of color, rushing by headed god knows where. It's hard to make out exactly what's going on out there as my eyes refuse to focus, but when my body goes into full on relapse there's nothing that I can do.

The hospital is a cold, dreary place. Ancient brick walls surrounding bed after bed filled with patients resting away whatever it is that ails them, laying in wait for a day when they can feel normal again.

For many of us, that day might never come.

At least it feels that way.

I look down through blurred vision and a foggy mindset and I see a body that refuses to do as it's told. Hands that refuse to stop twitching, a voice that refuses to express the words in my head, and legs that just don't work the way they did five days ago. I look down and I find it increasingly difficult to see the light at the end of this tunnel.

There's an old woman that I see every day in the common room. She sits at her table, slowly eats her food, and spends the next several hours staring off at nothing. I see her and I can't help but wonder how long she's been here. Has she been stuck in here for so long that the idea of doing anything other than silently staring seems like a waste? Is her silent stoic glare anything other than the endgame of my attempts to find focus in the cars in the distance beyond the pane of glass in my room? Is it any different than what I do when I watch her as she stares? Is this my future? Will I one day end up so lost in my own body that my days will be spent staring at a wall for hours on end?

If that day ever comes, please put a bullet in my head.

Just end it.

Eternal, unconscious darkness will always be preferable to the torment of constant boredom.

I'd Rather Find Blood in my Stool

The world of online hook ups was something completely foreign to Carl. It was all too simple. Swipe right, it's a match, get your dick sucked.

It felt sad.

It felt like desperation.

But who the fuck is Carl to judge anyone? He up and married the first woman that ever showed him any sort of attention and then spent the next 12 years pretending that she wasn't cheating on him, no matter how deep into his face she was mushing it. He sat there and took it for over a decade, all in the name of misplaced compassion and the fear of never being likable enough for anyone to ever want him. It was seeded deep and in his mid thirties he knew that it was something that he could never get passed.

But what's a man to do, really? Your hand can only get you so far and two years is a long time. But Carl wasn't exactly good with women. Misplaced dedication to the wrong person in your sexual prime can do that to someone. Carl was awkward with women, he never knew what to say. Sure, there are women who find that endearing. Carl's awkward personality may very well be the perfect fit for some lucky lady out there, but at thirty five years old it feels like it's too late to keep waiting. His time is in the past. Everything is exhausting and sexual pursuit is only going to stress him out more than he already is. No, Carl needs something simple. Something he once called sad and desperate now seems to be his only hope.

It's fitting.

Carl's both sad *and* desperate.

As he pulled out his phone and opened the app, Carl laughed at the absurdity of himself using such a thing. He was better than this, right? He didn't need some matchmaking application to tell him who he should be attracted to. Besides, it's not like these things use some sort of elaborate algorithm that succinctly sets you up with your perfect match, it just checks if the people you like liked you back and tells you to go fuck each other.

He wasn't better than this and he knew it. He spent twelve soul crushing years living in a world where sex had become nothing more than something someone else allowed him to do. He never got the chance to flourish, to experiment. He never got to have as much fun as every single person around him seemed to be having. That's what loyalty will bring you folks: Regret. Long nights sitting in the dark thinking about what could have been and touching yourself to the thought of someone, *anyone* touching you back.

Not only was Carl not too good for this, this was exactly what he needed. He needed a chance to get out there and have a little fun. Some non committal, care free fun. Carl deserved a chance to be happy.

As soon as Carl opened the app, he was asked to set up an account. He entered an e-mail, a password, the regular stuff. Once that was complete, it was time to set up his account.

Name: Carl
Location: California
About Me: Hi, I'm Carl. I'm new to this, so take it easy on me, okay? I'm not sure what to write, so I'll probably come add more here later.
Occupation: Writer

When it asked for a picture, Carl used the camera on his phone to take a selfie right then and there. He fiddled with his hair a bit to get it as right as he could and he snapped a picture.

It was awful. The flash washed out his skin and smoothed away any sort of texture therein while simultaneously highlighting the tiny hairs poking through his unshaven face. The shadows contrasted his hair in such a drastic way that it made it look greasy and unwashed. Carl wasn't the most handsome man in the world, but this was just ridiculous.

So he tried again. He snapped a few more selfies and after some time decided to look through his old pictures of himself and pick out a good one. He dug through folder after folder in his phone's memory until he found the perfect picture. When he uploaded it and the app asked if he would like to upload another.

"No," Carl said to himself, "I don't think I will."

With the setup all out of the way, it was time to get started. Picture after picture of beautiful women found their way to his screen. It was like a buffet of women who would never give him the time of day out in the real world, all hanging out and waiting for his approval.

"Let's see," Carl said, looking over the top of his glasses like an old man, "I swipe right if I like them, left if I don't. That seems easy enough."

Dana, 34
20 miles away
Cashier

I like boozing and abusing!
J/K, I'm just a fun loving
girl looking for a good time!

Swipe right.

Bruna, 28
14 miles away
Waitress

Polyamorous love group
looking for our number 4

Swipe left

Betty, 36
5 miles away
Small business owner

The world is a scary place
Lets cower away from it
together!

Swipe right

Audrey, 35
2 miles away
Writer

Tell me a scary story and
I'll tell you what turns
me on

Swipe right

Martha, 31
7 miles away
Whatever I want!

I am against the willful mutilation
of baby boys in the name of
archaic religious practices.
If you have a foreskin then
swipe right, otherwise, swipe
left and take your mutilated cock
elsewhere!

Swipe left

Toni, 30
3 miles away
Proud mother
I am the proud mother of three
boys looking for a more than
a casual hookup. If you don't
like kids then swipe left
because my boys are my life

Swipe left

A few swipes was all it took for Carl to get into the groove of it all. It started to feel like a game; he was the decider. He got to choose which of these women were desirable and which would remain forever without his loving attitude and charming face. Kids? That's a swipe left. Weirdo? Send that shit to the left pile, baby! Simply looking for a hook up? A one night stand? A dick to suck for a little while? Let me help you on over to the right with a SWIPE!

It was fun, sure, but Carl couldn't help but notice that he wasn't finding any matches. Apparently none of the women he liked were liking him back. Then again, he signed up for the app less than ten minutes ago, there's a good chance that none of these women have even seen his profile yet. Carl has a problem with looking at the worst possible angle with any situation. He's a pessimist and a cynic through and through, so the thought of anything going well for him in any situation tends to get lost underneath the pile of unchecked negativity that swirls through his thoughts at a near constant clip.

Soon enough, Carl reached the end of the line. No more potential matches meant no more swiping. He could extend his search radius to reach a further supply of sex candidates, but he didn't feel he needed that just yet. Put the phone down, give it some time and his matches would start to show themselves. He was confident it would happen for him. It had to. This might be his last chance.

The Forest Provides

The sun shone through the trees like a thousand fingers of light reaching out to the forest floor. Bonnie smiled as she watched a soft breeze breathe life into her surroundings. Frankie, a stout Australian Shepard that refused to leave Bonnie's side snapped his jaws playfully at the fluttering leaves as they danced their way to the ground in what felt like a choreographed reminder that Autumn was in full swing.

"Calm down Frankie!" Bonnie said with a bit of a laugh and a sing song lilt to her voice, "You don't want to tire yourself out before we get there!"

Frankie looked back at Bonnie and with a wag of his tail he trotted back to where she had called out to him. This all had become daily routine for the two friends. It had started out as a bit of exploration in the woods, just a woman and her dog making a day out of searching for whatever they might find. But it all changed when they found something that would put an end to all of that. Months of searching for nothing without a clear goal in mind had finally come to an end once they finally found the exact thing that they didn't realize they were looking for. A Simple clearing in the middle of the woods was all it took to make them rethink the world that they lived in. The glade was lovely, but it felt like something more. Everything beyond its boundaries seemed like a fleeting thought from the past where memories go to hide from the moment.

"We're almost there," Bonnie said as Frankie started to whine with impatience, "No need for all of that!"

The glade was always beautiful at this time of day. The golden grass that spread from edge to edge reflected the light of the afternoon sun with such brilliance that at times it felt more like a living painting than a simple forest clearing. The trees that marked its perimeter seemed to encase it all in a perfect circle. The denseness of the forest beyond was so thick that even the idea of light refused to penetrate its dark exterior. It felt confusing at times; recalling exactly where they came into the glade became impossible when they examined its edges and found that it looked pretty much the same from every angle. No matter though, whatever side they left through always seemed to be the right way since they always managed to find their way back home.

After they stepped through the trees and took in all of the glade's magnificence, Frankie did as he always did. He darted straight for the center of the clearing and sniffed at the reason the two decided to start making their daily trips out here.

"Bark!" Shouted Frankie as he looked back at Bonnie wondering what was taking her so long.

"I'm coming, I'm coming!" Bonnie called as she made her way to Frankie's side and laid out a blanket on which to sit down.

Frankie pawed at a patch of dirt at the exact center of the glade as if he was trying to uncover what was underneath. Bonnie pulled him back as she leaned forward. In her hand, Bonnie held a small broom which she used to brush away the dirt on the top of the patch revealing what Bonnie had come to refer to as "The Asshole of the Forest."

No one thinks of a fleshy asshole embedded in the ground in the middle of a forest as natural, but here we are. When she first found it, Bonnie was concerned. Assholes, normally, are connected to asses, which in turn are connected to bodies. Judging by the size of *this* asshole, the body it might've been connected to would have been enormous, but upon closer inspection, Bonnie found that it was attached only to the ground. No secret buried giants, no previously undiscovered mega-fauna, just the ground and its asshole.

"Bark!" Shouted Frankie again as he danced around in an over exuberant fit of excitement, "Bark, bark, bark!"

"Patience!" Bonnie barked back, shooting Frankie a stern look causing him to sit down and wait patiently like a good dog.

With a smile on her face, Bonnie reached her hand deep into the asshole. It twitched about at first as if it felt uncomfortable, but soon enough it was good to go. The twitching calmed down as Bonnie reached deeper and deeper. She grabbed about for a moment before pulling her arm back out, the asshole trembling in relief as her hand popped free, now holding a fresh new rawhide bone.

"Are you ready?" Bonnie asked as she turned her attention to Frankie.

Ever the good boy that he was, Frankie began to wag his tail with excitement while remaining in his patiently seated position. He watched intently as Bonnie pulled her hand back, winding up, getting ready to let it rip.

"Go get it!" She shouted as she threw the bone across the glade.

Bonnie watched with a smile as Frankie ran at full speed after the bone. He had to look around for a moment before he found it and brought it back to Bonnie's side where he lay down on her blanket and gnawed away at his newly acquired rawhide. Bonnie scratched Frankie behind his ear and Frankie returned the gesture by turning back to her and nuzzling his head into her lap for a moment before getting back to his bone.

Bonnie reached back into the asshole. It twitched again as it acclimated itself to the prodding and as soon as it was ready Bonnie reached deep. She fiddled about again before finding what she was looking for. As she pulled her hand back to the surface the asshole began to pulsate as if it didn't want to let Bonnie pull out.

"Eeeeeeasy," Bonnie said with a quick pat to the asshole's rim, "Easy now."

With a collected mindset and a few amiable, gentle tugs of her arm, the asshole calmed down and seemed to relax as Bonnie continued to gently pull towards the surface. As more of her arm came free, the asshole seemed to smooth over, all of its wrinkles seemingly disappearing as what was coming from within pulled closer and closer to the surface. The asshole stretched wide and seemed to come close to full on prolapse as Bonnie's hand finally came free, carrying with it a picnic basket filled to the brim with the most delicious looking breads and cheeses and cold-cuts.

Fruits and treats galore!

The asshole looked beat up, but Bonnie knew it would be okay. It had seen much more damage than this and it always seemed to go back to normal in a matter of minutes.

Bonnie began to dig through her newly acquired picnic basket. She pulled out a little bit of everything and began to fill her belly with the fruits of her labors. This wasn't her first asshole picnic and it certainly wouldn't be her last.

Bonnie took in her surroundings. The autumnal glade was beautiful, Frankie was happy, the asshole was slowly regaining its tautness, the food was good, all was well.

The world can be a weird place.

Bonnie was happy.

A Tribute to Dame Helen Mirren
(Journal Entry c. 2019)

I feel like if I ever went to a salon to have my asshole bleached, I would be actively developing the worst day in another person's life.

If I were to guess, I would say that I could count the times I have looked at my own asshole on one hand. Be it through a mirror or a camera or whatever. The times in my life where I have felt the need to take a gander at the old brown eye have been few and far between.

And with good reason.

It's been quite some time since I've seen it, but if memory serves me properly, it was quite the sight. As Adam Sandler once said, "I looked at my asshole in the mirror today. It blew my fucking mind." I can't quite describe it to you in detail, but I have a vague recollection of the color, and that alone would be enough to get me rethinking my own life choices. Color is a hard thing to describe. Sure, green, red, yellow, those are all pretty simple. If you see some green grass, you would describe it as green. Mixing together the basics isn't all that hard either. Greenish yellow? Sure, you can picture that no problem. It's easy to comprehend. It's when you start to mix together colors that shouldn't go together where you start to get lost. Brownish blue. I mean, sure, your brain can put together something for you to visualize, but it would never really be the proper color being described to you. You really need to see it.

Since I can't really give you a color and I don't trust your brain to accurately portray for you what I would be trying to put across, I guess I need to compare it to something. If I would compare it to anything, I would compare it to the look of old ham that gets left out and goes bad. But not quite the rotting away, covered in mold sort of bad. More along the lines of ham that is a few days passed its sell by date and left in a humid room. It's that grayish pink color with a weird film of rainbow slicked across its surface.

Mind you, this all comes from what is likely a decades old memory at this point. For all I know, the years could have been good on my asshole. My memory could be entirely inaccurate. My asshole could have been a sight to see that my memory has altered to cover up for the fact that I embarrassingly held a mirror between my legs to take a look at the place from where my farts are expelled. It could have been an absolute beauty that over the years has aged gracefully, like Dame Helen Mirren.

But of course, my memory could be completely accurate and time may have only painted a portrait of filth onto a canvas of absolute depravity.

I am too scared to check.

I don't think I want to know.

My asshole has never been the center of conversation, so I don't think it really matters. I have no intention to get an asshole bleaching, or an asshole waxing, or anything asshole related really. Going to the bathroom not withstanding.

Your welcome, asshole bleachers of America.

You won't have MY asshole in front of you any time soon. You can continue your good work for now.

Godspeed.

Psychiatrist's Office

On TV, they always seem to make psychiatrists offices as brown as they possibly can. Brown leather chairs and couches, deep brown desks; the walls are brown, hell, half the time the doctors themselves are wearing nice brown slacks under a brown jacket with brown patches on the elbows. They always have neatly coiffed brown hair and glossy brown glasses giving aid to their pensive brown eyes. Seriously, what is it with all the brown? I assume it's because brown is such a neutral color and a psychiatrists role is to listen before taking sides. They're neither an ally nor an enemy. They aren't listening to their patients with a black and white outlook, their thoughts are purely brown. Their ideas are brown. The help that falls out of their mouth is brown.

I remember being a kid and watching Jason Seaver, the stalwart father of Mike and Ben from the television series Growing Pains doling out heaps of advice to his sons inside his office, and guess what color that office was. Guess what color Dr. Seaver's hair was. Brown. All of it. It was all brown. What color was Lucy Van Pelt's psychiatry booth where she offered questionable advice to the rest of the Peanut's gang for five cents a head? Brown! Of course it was brown! Psychiatry is a brown science!

So, you have to be asking yourself: Why is this person rambling incoherently about the color of psychiatry offices right now rather than letting me know who he is or what he is doing or where this story is going?

This a fair question.

My mind tends to wander; all the time, actually. If I'm out grocery shopping, I may think to myself 'Self, you need to go get some brussels sprouts and then get the hell out of this place.' but as I make my way to the produce section, I find myself in frozen foods laughing at the Kid's Cuisines. I'm what you might call a scatterbrain. I'm always aware that things are going on, but I'm not always aware of whether or not I'm keeping up with what I need to be keeping up with. Take right now for example. I'm supposed to be doing something, but I'm not really sure what it is. I'm sitting here, thinking about fictional psychiatry offices, losing myself in my own thoughts and remembering obscure TV dads and cunty little girls who are constantly bullying the titular character and have the gall to offer up advice to the rest of the gang about what they need to do to get their lives together.

Man. Peanut's was a weird comic.

"Ted, are you with me?" Came the all too familiar voice of Dr. Browning.

"I... What?" I answered, confused.

"I asked you how your week went and you have just been staring at the table for two minutes."

There it is.

"Oh. Oh, yea, my week's been fine." I answered, somewhat embarrassed by my lapse of thought.

"Good, good." Dr. Browning said as she scribbled into her notebook, "So there were no exploding head fantasies?"

The question caught me off guard. I'm not really sure why though, the whole reason I started seeing Dr. Browning was to get help curbing my head explosion fantasies. You see, every once in a while, during my regular, waking, everyday life I will look at someone and their head will explode. I have no control over it, it just happens. There's no pathology to it; I don't need to know the person; age, race, gender: all meaningless here. If your head was supposed to explode at that given moment, by god your head was about to explode.

They didn't really explode of course. They wouldn't be called head explosion fantasies if the heads actually exploded. Then they would just be head explosions. A head explosion reality. A place where at any random time for no discernible reason, one's head may explode into a red mist of blood and brain matter. The fantasies aren't fun, they're terrifying and I could only assume that as a reality it would be equally as terrifying.

"Ted." Came Dr. Browning's voice once more, "You're doing it again."

"Huh?" I responded, quickly looking up from the glass I seemed to have been staring at again, "Doing what?"

"You're staring off again."

"Oh," I said, "I didn't realize."

Like I said, my mind wanders.

"Okay," Dr. Browning said, "let's try and reset. Why don't you explain to me exactly what it is that you need me to help you with?"

"Um," I started, "You want me to tell you why I'm seeing you?"

"Yes, please, explain to me exactly what it is that has been going on in that head of yours."

"But I've been seeing you for five months. You know why I'm here, it's the exploding heads thing."

"Yes, of course, But what I want you to do is to go over it all out loud with me. I think if your mind is focused on that for a bit it will help with keeping your mind from wandering."

"Okay," I answered with a somewhat uneasy tone, "I guess that makes sense."

I didn't really think it made sense. I pay Dr. Browning by the hour; I want to get as much help as I can in that time. I really want my money's worth. Reiterating what we have been talking about for months really felt like a cheap, poorly disguised ploy to get me to pay for another hour of therapy. She was nickel-and-diming me here.

That's not to say that it hasn't happened before; about a month back I caught her scribbling pictures onto her notepad while I was talking. I only caught a glimpse of it, but I'm fairly certain that she was drawing me; and then some time before that I caught her sleeping. She denies it of course. She said it was a 'Delusional fantasy'; that it manifests out of the paranoia that I am always telling her about.

Well you know what I think?

I think that she heard me mention that I sometimes feel a little paranoid about the mailman or my neighbors or whatever and decided then and there that this was a good opening to bilk this poor crazy sap for all he is worth. The safe is open, man! Wide open! All that money inside waiting for someone to reach through and grab it. To steal from me under the guise of a doctor who is selflessly working day after day to make me better. Lying directly to my face with every word spoken throughout our entire time together. None of it was the truth, she kept the truth hidden. Just under the surface where she thought I couldn't see it. She wanted to cut off my paranoia and treat it as an illness and convince me that I'm crazy because she knows that even though my paranoia was her opening, it was also my key. A key I hold without even realizing it. A key that can open up all of the lies that she has locked away and reveal to me that she has been out to get my money all along!

I will not stand for it!

Just as I decided I would no longer stand for it, it happened. Dr. Browning looked me directly in the eyes. Her smile slowly faded away as she looked down and wrote something onto her notepad. As she looked back up to me and her head began to swell to cartoonish proportions. Her eyes bulged grotesquely out of her skull with enough force and separation to knock her glasses down to the floor. Her lips blistered over as blood filled mounds swelled up onto them. And just as quickly as it began, it all ended with a comically quiet 'pop' as her head exploded into a viscous mist of red colored matter flying violently in all directions and coating everything it touched in a bath of blood, brain matter, and skull fragments.

One of her blown out eyeballs hit me right in the chest.

In our sessions, Dr. Browning has told me that the best thing for me to do during a head explosion is to try as hard as I can to keep calm and remind myself that it isn't real. It's all just a figment of my imagination. A way for my brain to purge itself of all the paranoia, distrust, and all around negative energy that I keep trapped inside of it.

It's true. It's all an illusion. None of it is actually happening to me. But in the moment, when you can feel the warmth of the inside of someone's body splashed across your face, it gets a little hard to imagine that it isn't real. It may not actually be there, but in my head, that 98.6f brain matter that is pulsating on my lips feels just about as real as a dream. The sensation of someone's inside's sloughing down my face right now is as real as it gets, and trust me; it's not something that I want to be feeling.

"It just happened, didn't it?" Dr. Browning asked, her voice reaching deep into my thoughts and ripping me back into reality.

I shook my head quickly in disbelief, as if I were trying to shake off the viscera that wasn't actually there. I looked around the room and quickly took note of all the surfaces once covered in blood, now all as clean as the day they were purchased.

"Huh?"

"My head just exploded," Dr. Browning said matter-of-factly, "Didn't it?"

"It did."

"Can you tell me what was happening just prior to it?" She asked, "What was going through your head?"

I contemplated this for a moment.

"Well," I said, "Nothing out of the ordinary."

Sex Sells?

"Hey!" the voice called out to me, "What in the sweet name of FUCK do you think you are doing?"

Confused, I look around myself, assuming the words had been intended for someone else. It was a safe assumption too, seeing as how with the exception of breathing and sitting silently, I was doing nothing of note.

"Me?" I ask

"Yea fucking you! What in the hell do you think you're doing?"

"Well, I'm pretty sure I'm sitting silently on my front porch and enjoying the light breeze that's flowing through the neighborhood. Is there some sort of problem with me enjoying the breeze?"

He ponders this for a moment before throwing up his arms in an act of sheer confusion.

"Listen, buddy, you can enjoy the fucking breeze all you want," his tone is firm and forceful, "but when you're doing it with your hard prick in your hand, people might want to ask you a few questions about it!"

"What?!" I ask, slowly lowering my gaze towards my lap.

Well, he isn't making things up. I do indeed have what he so delicately referred to as my 'hard prick' in my hand. I mean, I clearly wasn't aware of it, but that's neither here nor there. Nothing that comes out of my mouth now will placate this gentleman's ire.

"Oh... Goodness..." I say as I release my grip from my erect penis.

As one might expect (and I don't say this to boast) it stands at attention as if I hadn't yet released it. As I rise to my feet, it remains in position, altering only slightly in regards to direction, finding itself pointed directly at the angry gentleman.

He glares at it, dumbfounded and disgusted, with a look on his face that betrays a hint of something hiding behind his contempt. Possibly a glint of desire.

It's probably just my imagination, but imagination or not, if this gentleman, the one standing in front of me and staring with contempt into my genitals began to lick his lips without a hint of shame, I wouldn't be surprised at all.

This man looks like the type of man who would jump at the shot to get his lips firmly placed around any and every erect cock he has ever come across.

Some might say he hides it well, but he doesn't.

"Listen," I say to the gentleman, "This is all a misunderstanding, sometimes I lose track of what I am doing and find myself in these kinds of situations."

"These kinds of situations?" The irate man shoots back, "The kind where you end up jerking your prick on your front porch for the whole neighborhood to see?"

"No, the kind of situations where I get myself into trouble." I answer.

"Sheila!" the irate man calls out to his unseen spouse, "Get the sheriff on the phone!"

"Sheila, no, please, wait!" I plead, "If you just let me get on the phone, I can have my pills by tomorrow. They keep me in check and we won't need to get the sheriff involved."

Since this unseen entity known as Sheila is out of sight and therefore out of mind, beyond my own comprehension, I have to work with the assumption that she has heard my pleas and decided to hold off on calling the sheriff. Of course, I will find out in no time that my assumptions are dead wrong, but I am still forced to work within them with my next few words. Lord knows I don't want to go back to the psych ward.

"It's just, I'm sorry, what's your name?" I ask him, hoping familiarity will help bring some brevity into the situation.

"Burt." He tells me matter-of-factly, the word bursting forth from his lips with all the delicacy of a wet fart.

"Okay, Burt, pleased to meet you." I tell him, "My name is Rudolf. I just moved into the neighborhood."

"Rudolf? What kind of kraut name is Rudolf?!"

"Well, it was my father's name, actually." I inform him, this time hoping to pull on his heartstrings by invoking the F word. I mean, maybe he has kids. Maybe he can understand.

"Was HE a kraut?" I guess being a kraut trumps being a father…

"He was born in Austria, if that is what you're asking…"

"That is EXACTLY what I was asking!" he says, turning back towards where I assume the aforementioned Sheila is hiding, "You hear that Sheila? Another god damned Kraut moving into OUR neighborhood and jerking off his delicious cock in front of OUR children!"

"Delicious?" I ask.

"What?"

"Nothing... Listen, Burt, if we could just leave the sheriff out of this, I'm sure we can all walk away from this unfortunate situation with smiles on our faces. Perhaps more."

Burt ponders this for a moment, all the while never taking his eyes away from my still fully exposed erection. He glares at it as my words penetrate him.

"Burt, we can make this go away." Burt's gaze rises up to meet mine, "Just say the word."

Burt stares deep into my eyes, understanding exactly what I'm alluding to but not quite understanding how to handle it. I can see him wonder; even fantasize in that short amount of time, what it might feel like in his mouth. How it might taste. Does he want to work for the ending that he desires, does he want to take charge over how my climax might come, or does he want to be passive in his endeavors? Does he want to suck it, or does he want to lay back and have the sucking take place for him? He knows he wants it. We both know he wants it. But he can't quite comprehend why he wants it. Burt doesn't see himself as a homosexual. He hasn't come to terms with it and judging by his age and his demeanor, I doubt he ever will. But that's neither here nor there to me at this moment. I am simply preying on this poor closeted soul's insecurities in an attempt to avoid another year or so in the loony bin.

"Pull your pants up, son." He says, "The sheriff has a bit of a lead foot. Let's not force him to have to look at what you're showing off."

"Are you sure you want that?" I ask as my hands reach down for the waist of my pants. "I believe I have made myself clear in regards to what I am willing to do here."

"Sheila!" Burt screams, never breaking eye contact with me, "Make sure the sheriff knows he is dealing with a downright nut job here!"

"Sure thing Burt!" Calls a voice from a place unseen.

"And tell him to hurry! We don't want this one getting away!"

So much for hospitality.

As it seems, sex doesn't always sell.

The New Normal
(Journal Entry c. 2015)

Every day I wake up feeling like another piece of me has been stripped away and stomped deep into the wet mud that my life has become. My creativity is what has always made me who I am. It has always separated me from my peers and now I find it slipping away as I wake up every day into a body that is becoming less and less my own.

Do you understand what it feels like to not be able to feel parts of yourself?

Not just on the outside either. Some days, my memory feels as numb as my legs.

Some days, even worse.

You know that feeling that you get when you walk into a room and you look around and you can't for the life of you remember why exactly you went there in the first place? This is a constant occurrence on most of my days. I always have a bit of a lapse of memory here or there and it's something that I've gotten used to. It's become normal and that's fine. But some days, it's almost constant. It happens over and over and over where I just keep walking into rooms and forgetting what the whole point was in the first place.

It's something that I'll get used to, just like the lesser occurrences. One day, it will start and I'll be able to say "Shit, I guess it's just one of those days."

My long term memory has taken a hit too.

Sometimes, not all the time mind you, but sometimes, I'll try and remember my daughter's face from when she was a child and I just can't seem to do it. Unless it is a specific picture that I've looked at a thousand times, I just can't seem to picture it and it drives me insane. It makes me want to scream and cry all at the same time.

But I guess this is all just normal now.

Sgt. Tibbs

The other day after work, my cat talked to me. I had just worked a quadruple shift and I was dead tired; I've been told that hallucinations aren't all that uncommon during stints of extreme exhaustion, but this wasn't my first quadruple shift and it's never happened before.

Anyway, I sit down on my couch and tune my television to the local sporting event when Sergeant Tibbs, that's my cat, comes sauntering up onto the coffee table in front of me and starts talking to me.

"Hey Ted," he says to me, "You should kill yourself."

Needless to say, this took me by surprise. Cats aren't supposed to talk, and they definitely shouldn't be going around telling their owners to kill themselves.

"Why would you say that?" I asked, confused by this whole situation.

"Meow" Replied Sergeant Tibbs.

Now, this wasn't the answer I was expecting. Although I probably should have, considering he's a cat.

"Don't you do this to me, man!" I shouted at the cat.

"Meow." He replied.

That tiny little cat's natural call sent me into a fit of rage. He spoke. He looked me in my eyes and he told me to kill myself! Now he is going to sit there with his fuzzy little face and meow at me like nothing ever happened?! No! I wouldn't stand for it!

"Tibbs! I demand that you speak to me again!" I said in a calm and collected tone.

"Meow."

"CURSES!" I screamed as I put my fist as hard as I could through the glass top of my coffee table.

"Meow."

The shattered glass cut up my hand pretty badly. That's how I ended up here at the doctor's office. He says I am going to need around thirteen stitches to close up all of the open wounds. It's alright, my insurance should cover it.

Maybe I should see a psychiatrist too.

On Dreams
(Journal Entry c. 2015)

It's often said that dreams are the unconscious desires of the waking mind; those thoughts that we may be unwilling to vocalize, given life through our unconscious. Some believe a dream can be a way to purge out that which we know we shouldn't be bogging ourselves down with.

In reality, a dream can drudge up feelings and emotions that we may have been trying our damnedest to bury underneath the layers and layers of a facade that we've been building up over the years in order to hold back specifically what we are trying to hide from. A dream can take all the thoughts and feelings that you thought you had purged and lay them all out in front of you and remind you of a time that you will never be able to get back. They can give you a fleeting glimpse of what could have been and then without any sense of cognizance drop you back into your waking life where what you want is something that you know you can never have.

Some say dreams are a blessing. They say they can take our utmost desires, the one's that we can never truly or consciously obtain, and give them to us. Regardless of how real they might feel, the reality is that they simply are not.   Dreams have a bad habit of taking the real world and turning it into a nightmare in which your only reprieve comes with the dreaming world that is causing the waking nightmare to begin with. It seems that there's no rest for the dreamer. The dreamer will always see the world that they can never have and be constantly reminded that it's not going to happen for them.

Soulmates

"Hey now! You need to stop raping my wife!" The man called out from his bathroom.

"Honey, how many times do I have to tell you? Nobody's raping me." His wife answered, her voice filled with considerable aggravation, "Just because I'm out of your sight doesn't mean I'm going to be raped!"

"Yea, well," The man responded, "It doesn't mean you aren't going to get raped either."

Phlinda and Ghonny had always been a peculiar couple. Ever since the day they first met, twenty seven years ago in their high school gymnasium, they have rarely left each other's side. Some might look at twenty seven years of constant companionship as a blessing. Having someone by your side is always something of note. Others, however, might see twenty seven years as being far too long to be around someone. Neither of these thoughts is wrong, nor is either correct. It's simply a matter of taste. Some people enjoy prolonged exposure to the same person for years on end while others think the idea of it is a grotesque abomination that should be doused in kerosene and set aflame before it is able to mature into a general malaise that allows the exposure to occur. Phlinda and Ghonny both fall into the latter category.

So how, you might ask, did two people, two mature and intelligent human beings who are so adverse to this idea of a long term relationship end up in one that has lasted close to three decades? Well, the answer is quite simple, actually. You see, Phlinda and Ghonny are soulmates.

Many people hear the term soulmates and are immediately turned off to whatever weird conversation they happened to be having that resulted in its mention. They feel that if there's only one person out there for them, the chances of them actually finding their soulmate are so astronomical that it will most likely never happen. This is true. I don't know the numbers and I refuse to even attempt to do the math, but the fact of the matter is that the chances of actually finding your soulmate are significantly lower than the chances of waking up in the morning and finding a three pound glowing emerald lodged inside of your asshole. It's a strange comparison to make, so we had better not think any deeper into it.

Yes, the chances of actually coming across your soulmate are ridiculous. In all likelihood, it isn't going to happen for you. It likely isn't going to happen for me either. Or 99.99% of all the people that you or I have ever actually come into contact with. But for Ghonny and Phlinda, it happened. Against all odds, they found each other, and that is just something you don't want to piss away.

"Why, Ghonny, why does your mind always go to rape?" Phlinda asked

"Can you think of something worse happening to you?"

"At the moment, no."

"Exactly! What is worse than rape?!?" Ghonny asked

"Ghonny, we go over this every single night. There is never anybody here. I am never getting raped. Would you please just brush your fucking teeth and get to bed?!"

Ghonny, deflated, turned to the sink. He gave himself a quick look over in the mirror before opening up the medicine cabinet and pulling out his toothbrush and some toothpaste.

"You know, Phlinda, the day is going to come where I try to stop your rapist and you are going to be glad I did. You know why?"

"Why, Ghonny?" Phlinda asked with more than a hint of fatigue in her voice.

"Because he is going to be RAPING you!" Ghonny retorted as he poked his head out of the bathroom and jabbed a knowing finger at Phlinda.

"Who is going to be raping me?!" Phlinda shouted

"The RAPIST!" Ghonny bit back, "He is going to be on top of you, pumping away against your will, and you are going to be relieved that your husband of 27 years was there to call him out on his raping ways!"

Phlinda glared at Ghonny for a moment before lying back down and turning her body away from the blinding luminescence emanating from just behind Ghonny's blacked out face.

"Every fucking night." She sighed to herself.

"What was that?" Ghonny called from the bathroom, his mouth full of foamed up tooth paste

"I said hurry up and shut off that fucking light!"

Dad
(Journal Entry c. 2015)

My father is a good man. He may be gruff and generally hard to read, but he is without question a good man. The best example of a man I have ever known. I have watched him, every day of my life, do whatever it was at any given moment that he felt was the right thing to do in order to benefit his family. I think so highly of my father that I may have put him on a pedestal that I don't think I can ever live up to. I don't think I have done much to show him that I feel this way, but I assure you that this is how I feel.

I know my father loves me. I have always known that he loves me, but I have always gotten the impression that he doesn't particularly like me. I guess saying I have always felt this isn't entire accurate. There was once a time that I felt like we got along. In my youth I was heavily into athletics. I was never exactly good at them, I can count on two fingers the times that I genuinely felt that I was good at a sport, and even at those times I was surrounded by a team that made me look good. I was never good at the sports that I loved to play, but that wasn't the point. I played sports because I knew it made my dad happy. I enjoyed making him happy and I genuinely had a good time with him.

My father taught me many lessons in my life. Too many to count, really, and looking deep into myself I don't think that I have done him proud with what he taught me. There is one lesson that he taught me that has stuck with me for my entire life: I am not good enough. Now, you might look at that and think I mean something other than what I do. I am not saying this in a negative way. I'm not saying that he made me feel inferior in any way or anything like that, it's actually quite the opposite. For my entire life, no matter what I did, be it work in school or helping someone carry a large box, nothing I have ever done has been good enough in my father's eyes. I could always have done better, even if only a little bit. This idea has always made me have the need to take a good hard look at any given action that I take and ask myself if this is the best possible way to do it. It makes me look at my work in a way that I think is commonplace in artists and writers: My work is never good enough. I read back what I have written and I tell myself that it isn't good enough, forcing myself to go over it again and change what needs to be changed. Granted, this attitude has made actually completing my work and doing something with it extremely hard. If you find something that I have written and it looks complete, keep in mind that in my head, it never was.

My father is a complicated man who made my life a flat out misery at times, but I need it to be known that I would never ask for it any other way. I don't want some uninteresting TV dad, or some dead beat movie dad. I want MY dad. The man for whom I hold a love which I have never been able to find the proper way to express.

Bus Ride

Road construction tends to be an inconvenience to everyone involved. The workers risk their lives working dangerously close to active roadways and the drivers using the roads are forced to deal with constant traffic that can back up for miles. The only people who benefit from it are the fat cats in city hall using it as a platform on which to drive their re election campaign's.

Well, after it's all said and done we get some nice fancy new roads, a lovely new medium, and some fancy new low energy lights, but no one, and I mean NO ONE cares about all of that while they are sitting in traffic. All anyone can think about at that point is how the traffic is ridiculous and how it shouldn't be that way!

Well, it is that way.

It's loud, it's intrusive, it lasts for a long time, and there is nothing you can do about it.

All you can do is bitch and moan day in and day out until it ends.

I like to say that this is why I take the bus. So that I don't have to sit in traffic and complain about how long it takes me to get everywhere. I make that claim so I can feel aloof to all those jerks driving around in their cars and stressing about how long they are sitting in traffic and about how the road construction is going to put them into an early grave.

Reality is, I take the bus everywhere because I can't drive a car.

Not that I never could drive a car. I used to have a license. I used to drive everywhere. I loved driving. I prided myself on my ability to drive. I wasn't a NASCAR caliber driver or anything. There was nothing spectacular about the way I drove, but in the twenty years that I could drive, I never once got into an accident. I was never once issued a ticket. I have had people tell me that I drove like an old lady, but I don't care. I was safe god damn it!

Driving was a luxury that I never realized I loved until after it was taken away from me.

I don't really need to get into it here, but certain maladies as a result of certain ailments make driving a car an impossibility for me and as such, I am no longer a licensed driver.

It would be akin to drunk driving.

It would be dangerous.

So now I ride the bus. Every day I climb aboard that behemoth of a machine and sit with all of the people that I used to look down on.

Today, the bus is late.

Much like all of those complaining drivers that I was talking about earlier, the bus is caught up in the traffic that the road construction is causing and much like the stressed out driver in all of those cars, I am standing at the bus stop with a group of equally stressed out bus riders; none of us really knowing when we will arrive at our destination because none of us know when we will even be able to be on our way.

To make it all just a little bit worse, by turning and looking towards the oncoming traffic that is basically sitting at a standstill at this point, we all can see our bus. Old number 99, about 200 yards away, moving at a snail's pace on its way to pick us all up and slowly take us, at the very same pace, to where ever it is that we're headed.

It's a uniquely helpless feeling, watching your ride creep along the traffic over a ten minute period before it finally reaches you. But when it finally does, it's glorious.

Well, not so much glorious as mundane.

Sure, it's awesome that you can finally be on your way, but you just watched a bus creep along a 200 yard stretch of road over a period of ten minutes. Your prospects of arriving at your intended destination in a timely manner are all but null.

Regardless of that, I'm on the bus. I'm lucky enough to have found a seat and I'm on my way.

I recognize many of the faces here. When you ride the same route every day, you start to notice the same people who ride the same route. It's like my own little scummy family.

"Hey man," Comes a familiar voice, "How're you doing today?"

I look up and see that the familiar voice is coming from a woman who I recognize as Maria. A kind woman, albeit a bit loud, who is always ready to strike up a conversation with no one in particular. If you sat across from Maria, she would at the very least smile and say hello. At most, she would talk your ear off about whatever the hell she wanted.

Luckily, she wasn't talking to me.

"Oh," Answered Frank, a kindly old man who frequents the 99 as well, "I can't complain."

"That's good to hear." Answered Maria.

"Well," Frank started again, "I CAN complain, but I'm not going to today!"

The two share a laugh and look around the bus for an approval from the other passengers that never actually comes.

"So," Maria began after regaining her composure, "I have a few things to complain about."

"Oh?" Frank said, his eyes clearly begging Maria not to tell him about it.

"Remember how I told you I was pregnant?" Maria said, raising her voice in order to speak over the bus's roaring diesel engine.

"I do…" Frank answered, not sure he wanted to know where this was going.

"Well," Maria continued, "Yesterday, I woke up and my sheets were all wet, right?"

"…" Frank just stared. He clearly didn't want to hear where this was going.

"Well I thought it was piss when I first noticed it. But when I turned the lights on I saw that it was blood. All over my pants and my sheets."

"Oh god." Frank replied, visibly shook.

"I had a miscarriage all over myself!" Maria shouted over the engine to a chorus of disgusted groans from the rest of the bus.

"Jesus Christ lady!" Said an annoyed voice from the back of the bus.

"I know, right?" Maria called back, oblivious to his disgust.

"There are kids on the bus!" Shouted another voice, "We don't need to hear about your fucking miscarriage!"

"Well excuse me!" Maria responded in a seemingly upset tone, "I'm just trying to share my day with my friend here!"

Maria gestures to Frank who looks back at the rest of the bus with a look on his face that is begging the crowd to not turn on him.

"It doesn't matter WHO you were talking to! It's indecent!"

"Just stop!"

"I think I am going to throw up!"

The people on the bus were clearly starting to get aggravated and Maria's inability to grasp exactly why they might be upset was only stoking the fire.

Then it happened.

As I was watching it all unfold, Maria's head began to swell up in a grotesque manner. I could hear the fluids within as they began to boil. An air pocket behind her eye popped and a pillar of steam began to rush out before her entire head exploded with a cartoonish "POP!".

Blood and skull and brain matter went flying all over the bus, coating every surface in a slick, thick red mess. Her nose flew clear across the aisle and bounced comically off of Frank's forehead.

The passengers on the bus erupted into a screaming applause. Drivers who were caught up in traffic alongside the bus who had seen what happened clapped their hands in approval. A young girl skipped up to the front of the bus and laid a large bouquet of flowers onto Maria's headless corpse before turning to me and smiling the sweetest smile you ever did see. I lost myself in that smile and as I returned in kind, I slowly but surely realized that it was all an illusion.

No one's head had exploded.

There was no blood, no skull, no brain matter.

Maria was still in her seat, alive and well, defending her stance that miscarriage talk on the bus isn't that big of a deal and that this bus full of prudes needs to ease up.

Maybe she's right, I don't know. Perhaps we were all just being a bunch of prudes. Who am I to decide what is and isn't appropriate bus talk, right? I just vividly imagined a woman's head exploding to the delight of everyone.

Untitled Journal Entry
(c. 2015)

One more glass of water and it's back to bed.

Back to dreaming of a world where my existence matters. Where I'm surrounded by people who care about me and who care about what I have to say.
That's the gamble of dreaming. Once you wake up, you might never be able to get back.
Your ideal world could be lost forever within the unconscious mind's countless misfirings and electrical eccentricities.
Every desire in your body holds true there. A world you can never live in, created for you, BY you, in ways you can never really understand.
You see her face, you love her, but you don't recognize her. A fleeting glimpse of what could have been but possibly never was. A whole new reality of your own design over which you hold no control.

Is it real?

It sure feels real.

Which is exactly why its loss can feel so utterly devastating.

ERs, MRIs, and Other Assorted Acronyms

Prolonged dizziness, shaky unusable legs, blindness in the left eye, deafness in the left ear, numbness in the limbs, face, and tongue.

My symptoms were both numerous and concerning.

I remember the doctor in the hospital talking to me in the middle of a hallway, smugly trying to get me to describe to him which drugs I took to end up in the state I was in. I hadn't taken anything and his incessant prodding wasn't exactly putting me at ease. If anything it was causing me more stress, a state of mind that I would soon come to find out is likely what caused this particular exacerbation to begin with.

I remember sitting in that hallway wondering what the hell was going on. I had just sat in the waiting room, blind deaf and dumb, for six hours, waiting for anyone to just come out and call my name so that I could see a doctor who would make it all stop. The hallway was crowded, filled to the brim with what felt like every single sick and injured citizen of Alameda County that wasn't able to afford an insurance that would send them to any hospital other than the cheap public option.

Highland Hospital in Oakland California, serving the under-served with the best care they could afford since 1927.
I, of course, was no better than any of them. I had recently lost my job and in turn my insurance, leaving me destitute in the biggest time of need I have ever experienced in my life. We were all on the public dime, waiting patiently in a crowded hallway, hoping to find some sort of relief from what ever might be causing us discomfort.

I remember the nurse telling me that I might be in that hallway for a while. She told me that I should try going to sleep. The screaming homeless man who kept trying to walk in through the ambulance entrance some twenty yards down the hall made sure that wasn't going to happen. I was pretty on edge that night. Granted, I couldn't walk and I couldn't talk and the people paid to figure out why weren't exactly helping me, but I've always tried to take that with a grain of salt. They were charged with helping a lot of people, not just me. Shit takes time. That isn't to say that it wasn't frustrating.

After some time, the doctors decided that it would be best to keep me overnight in order to keep an eye on me. They moved me into a temporary room in a different hallway on the same floor. They all looked the same, these hallways. They seemed to be actively working to prevent me from recalling where in the hospital I had been taken. The blinding white walls contrasting with the deep black trim all packed together with the fact that my vision and hearing had gone stupid made my journey into my room feel like I was living inside of a waking nightmare.

I remember the room being small. Not much bigger than a large closet. They rolled the bed I was laying on right into the room leaving just enough space for the nurse to fit me with an IV so she could periodically wake me up throughout the night and check it. It's fine, she was just doing her job. I couldn't really sleep anyway. In normal situations I tend to sleep on my side, but in this dark unfamiliar hospital room, finding comfort in any position was impossible. That tied in with my newfound fear of accidentally tearing out the IV in my sleep and pulling a hunk of vein out alongside it and bleeding to death made finding sleep an impossibility.

Vertigo.

Severe Dehydration.

Stroke.

All possible diagnoses. That's what the doctor told me the next morning. He probably said more, I don't know. I could barely hear anymore. Hell, I could barely see. That could have been the screaming homeless man from the night before for all I know.

"We're going to move you upstairs now," The nurse told me as she disengaged the brakes on my hospital bed, "The doctor wants to check you into the inpatient facility until we know what's wrong"

"Bokay." I said through my numb face and tongue, "Bewank yoof bewwy motch."[3]

I was rolled carefully through the nightmare halls and into a freight elevator where I got to ride up to the sixth floor next to the food that would be provided to the rest of the patients upstairs.   They brought me into the room where I would spend the next week being poked and prodded by a menagerie of student doctor's and interns being taught how to narrow down the results of test after test after test until they can find a proper diagnosis. My first big medical problem and I got to be a guinea pig, not much different from a CPR dummy or one of those birthing dolls with the big stretchy vaginas.

After a week, they must have exhausted all other possibilities and narrowed it down to one diagnosis in particular. The diagnosis that I have learned not many doctors like to give. Diagnosing something that can be cured is one thing. They get to tell the patient that there is good

---

3   Translation: "Okay, thank you very much."

news. In my case, the only good news was that they might have an answer. A reason for my suffering.

There were just two more tests they needed to administer to make sure.

A lumbar puncture is more commonly known as a spinal tap. A specialized needle is inserted into the lumbar section of the spine, directly between two vertebrae. The needle is built to function in a way where it can extract pure, untouched spinal fluid without tainting the sample with any outside fluids. This means that the needle needs to remain inserted into the spine for a moment so the mechanism can be engaged and disengaged before it can be removed. It doesn't sound like much, really. Its just a moment, you wont even know it's happening. That's what they tell you. All you need to do is sit there and relax and it will all be okay!

Well it's pretty difficult to relax in that moment. Sure, the whole procedure probably lasted less than two minutes, but the fact that you can feel every inch of that needle as it slides in and out your central nervous system coupled with the knowledge that this is the student doctor's first time administering this procedure[4] wreaks havoc on the amount of stress you're feeling. Nervous about your nervous system. It would be poetic if it weren't so terrifying.

The student doctor did a good job. I still have feeling in my legs, for the most part. Any numbness in my legs is a result of my disease, not the procedure that found it. They only had to poke around my spinal column the one time, so that's good. I do, however, occasionally feel a twinge of pain where the needle went in, but I'm not entirely sure that actually has anything to do with the procedure itself.

The second procedure was far less terrifying on paper. In practice, it is one of the most horrible experiences of my life, and soon enough I would be needing this procedure once every few months. An MRI uses a magnetic resonance field to take pictures of the inside of your body that are able to be viewed in three dimensions. It is honestly a marvel of modern technology. As a concept alone it's like something that came right out of the golden age of science fiction, described in great detail by the likes of Robert Heinlein or Isaac Asimov. The final step of futurist thinking.

I wasn't thinking about any of this when they put a cage over my head that would prevent me from being able to move around too much. The amazing results of what the machine could do were the furthest thing from my thoughts as they slid me inside and turned it on. My hearing was still all but gone at that point, but that wasn't enough to

---

4   I feel like this is the kind of information best kept from the patient, but I didn't go to medical school, so what do I know?

keep the loud clanging of the machine's inner workings out of my head. It sounds like an old 56k modem mixed with two idiots beating the shit out of an old washing machine with baseball bats. Like Robbie the Robot butt fucking an exhaust vent on the side of the C-57D in the upper atmosphere of some Forbidden Planet. It's okay though, it only lasts about an hour and a half. Those ninety minutes feel nothing like ninety minutes. You can watch Frankenstein in seventy minutes. Ghost in the Shell clocks in at eighty three minutes, but that movie just flies by. Ninety minutes in an MRI machine is a slog. It drags. It's ninety minutes that feel like three hours. Like watching the 1990 comedy Ski School[5].

After those ninety minutes passed, I was pulled from the machine by the technician who had put me in there in the first place. He was looking over some papers as I was transferring into the wheelchair that had brought me into the room.

"Tho," I started, still unable to speak like a human being, "Anthy goothd newth?"[6]

"Hmm?" He said as he looked up over the top of the papers, "Oh, I'm not allowed to discuss any of what I see with you. That's for the doctor."

"Oh," I said, trying not to show my disappointment in having to wait, "Noth worrieth."[7]

"Tell me," The tech said, "Have you ever heard of Multiple Sclerosis?"

And that, friends, is how I found out that I had an incurable disease that from that day forward would negatively affect almost every aspect of my life until the day I die.

---

5   Ski School clocks in at 89 minutes in length, but poor pacing and a
      meandering story make it feel like it's much, much longer.
6   Translation: "So, any good news?"
7   Translation: "Oh, no worries."

They Took Away His Dreams

The open road is never something to be trifled with. Endless stretches of nothing in all directions periodically dotted with the faintest signs of civilization can be both scary and dangerous. You can get lost in the banality of it all. Highway hypnosis can take hold and trick you into thinking that you've somehow slipped into one of those dimensions beyond, or a dream-state that forbids you from ever waking up.

Thankfully, there exist reminders along the way whose sole purpose seems to be to assure you that you aren't alone out here.

Life exists.

The world exists.

You are living in it, whether you remember it or not.

A restaurant here, a gas station there. A whole world of questions regarding who operates these havens of sanity and where they come from ignites in your brain and reminds you that you need to stop and take a shit.

"It's 3:30 AM," The radio says as Jacques turns off towards the next exit, "and you know what that means! It's time for everyone's favorite show: Celebrity Songs! The show where we play the songs that celebrities recorded despite no one asking for them or even hearing about them! First up, we've got Frivolous Pursuit, recorded in 1994 by none other than the star of the 1987 Stanley Kubrick classic Full Metal Jacket, Private Joker Himself, Matthew Modine! So sit back folks, let us take you away to another..."

"Ugh..." Jacques groans to himself as he reaches down and turns off the radio.

Jacques considers himself a patient man. A real go with the flow kind of guy. When the world throws him a curve ball, he leans into it and takes it on the shoulder. Normally, the idea of Matthew Modine singing a song that no one asked for would appeal to him, but unfortunately for Mr. Modine, this moment wasn't exactly one Jacques was proud of. Jacques's need to empty his colon currently supersedes his desire for new experiences. Perhaps when his bowels have been sufficiently moved he could once again appreciate the world as it occurred to him. For now, his focus was on setting a quick moment aside and keeping it for himself. There's no shame in that.

"Just get out of the car," Jacques said to himself, "Go take a shit, and be on your way. No need to cause any trouble."

Jacques stared out through his windshield at a man standing behind the cash register inside of the building. The man was staring back at Jacques.

"Weird." Jacques said when he noticed the man staring at him.

When it's 3:30 in the morning and you're working the register at a Burger King in the middle of nowhere, you tend to stare at the things that seem to drift into your life. Maybe it's a truck driver passing through who decided to stop in for a quick bite before continuing on his way off to wherever it is that he might be headed. Maybe it's a family passing through on their way to wherever needing an early morning bathroom break. The who of the situation is inconsequential, really. When you work in the middle of nowhere serving nothing to nobody, the very idea of something different grabs your attention and forces you to watch. It may take a moment before you realize that it's real. That it isn't another hallucination that your brain conjured up to curb your unending loneliness. This is real, man. This is someone tangible, a physical being who is here to share your space with you and to talk to you and to remind you that you are indeed a human being, worthy of recognition.

"Alright Pierre," The cashier said to himself as he watched Jacques walk through the door, "This is your chance to shine, don't fuck it up."

A chime sounded as Jacques entered the building and triggered the sensor that's attached to the door. The sound filled the silence of the room and brought in a sense of life that hadn't been felt in hours.

"Good morning," Pierre said with a smile, "Welcome to Burger King. How can I help you today?"

"Where's the bathroom?" Jacques answered, barely acknowledging him.

"Gotta take a shit?" Pierre asked.

"I do..." Jacques answered as he stopped dead in his tracks and looked up at Pierre, "Is that really something that you should be asking your customers?"

"Well..." Pierre started to say as a frown stretched across his face, "Shit!"

Realizing the error of his way, Pierre pulled a revolver out from under the counter. Jacques could see its heft as Pierre lifted its weight up over the counter and placed the barrel against his temple.

Click

Pierre pulled the gun away from his head and looked at it inquisitively for a moment before placing it to his temple again.

Click Click Click

Pulling it away from his head again, Pierre took another look, desperate to figure out what was wrong. For a moment, he just couldn't seem to figure out why it wasn't firing. He looked down the barrel; nothing was blocking it. He looked at the hammer; pulling like normal.

Then it hit him.

"Oh for Christ's sake Pierre," He said to himself as he turned his attention back to Jacques, "I'm sorry sir, this should only take a moment."

Pierre held up one finger to Jacques, indicating that it would indeed only be one moment. He reached under the counter again and pulled out a box of bullets.

"Jesus Christ!" Jacques finally said as he watched Pierre fumble about with the revolver's many moving parts, "Are you trying to kill yourself?"

"Company policy." Pierre answered without looking up from the gun, "This is easier than having to deal with the paperwork involved with a customer complaint."

"Burger King has a *suicide* policy?!" Jacques said with an incredulous tone as he watched Pierre calmly load the cartridges into the pistol and once again place the barrel against his temple, "Wait, stop!"

"Sir," Pierre said as he looked up at Jacques, "I could get fired if I don't follow protocol."

"I'm not going to complain," Jacques said as he looked down at Pierre's name tag, "Okay, Pierre? You don't have to worry about losing your job. I promise you that I won't complain."

"You promise?" Pierre said as he started to pull the gun back down away from his head, "Well that's a relief. I would hate for the janitor to have to clean up the mess when he comes in."

"Yea, that would be a shame." Jacques said, relieved, "Now why don't you put the gun away and point me towards the bathroom. You were right all along. I DO have to take a shit."

"I knew it." Pierre said with a smile as he put the gun and the box of bullets away under the counter.

Pierre pointed in the direction of a hallway off to Jacques' right, indicating that was where the bathroom was located. Jacques smiled and turned to go into the bathroom as the smile quickly faded from Pierre's gaze and he turned to face forward again in an almost robotic like motion, returning to his duties having satisfied his daily customer quota.

***

The bathroom was quiet. Eerily so. The silence mixed with the cleanliness and the faint odor of bleach and ammonia gave the room an otherworldly feel. Jacques walked passed a line of urinals that hung from the wall in a way that seemed to be begging any and all passers-by to piss in them. He couldn't help but feel bad for them as he stepped into the closest toilet stall and locked the door behind him.

"This should be nice." Jacques weirdly said to himself as he unbuckled his belt and sat down onto the toilet.

Jacques let loose. He let the filth flow out of himself at breakneck speed. He smiled to himself with each splashdown, content in the fact that he had managed to pull off the highway in a timely manner and relieve himself somewhere other than in his pants.

"Psst..."

He wasn't quite sure whether or not he had actually heard it, so Jacques decided to ignore it. It wasn't real. His mind was playing a trick on him. That's okay, it's happened before. He could just ignore it so that can go ahead and finish up his business and be on his way.

"Psst..."

Jacques continued to nervously stare forward at the back of the stall door, pretending that he couldn't hear the beckoning sounds coming from the next stall. Jacques was well aware that truck stop bathrooms were havens for a certain kind of deviancy. The sort of acts that would be perfectly acceptable in a good portion of the civilized world but were now being perpetrated by those who despise their own feelings. Men who can't accept themselves in the light of day around their loved ones, so they act out in the shadows with willing, tight-lipped strangers who find themselves in the same situation. A moral conundrum that shouldn't exist. The beckoning from the next stall hadn't done much more than remind Jacques that he was now in a world where hushed whispers beckon with promises of silent pleasure. He took this reminder to heart and promised himself that he wouldn't allow himself to be sucked into that world.

At least this stall was fully in tact. Not a glory hole in sight.

"Hey, psst!" The voice whispered.

"Hello?"

Jacques answered this time. Once could be coincidence, but twice could... Also be a coincidence, but Jacques answered anyway.

"Passing through, or planning to stay?" Asked a voice from the next stall.

"I'm... I'm sorry," Jacques stammered, "I'm trying to use the bathroom, so if you could just..."

"Wanna see a freak show?"

"Do I want to see a..." Jacques took a moment to process, "Is that... Code?"

"Code?" The voice asked, confused, "What kind of code?"

"You know," Jacques answered, "Truck stop code. You asked if I wanted to see a freak show. Is that code for something?"

"Code for what?" The voice said, still confused.

"I don't know," Jacques responded, his voice filled with impatience, "Like, does it mean you want to suck my dick?"

"What?!" The voice said, aghast.

"Truck stop code!" Jacques shouted, suddenly filled with shame, "I'm not propositioning you! I'm just looking for clarification!"

"Well," The voice said, no longer whispering, "*To clarify*, I am not speaking in code. I asked if you wanted to see a freak show because I wanted to know if you would like to see my freak show."

"Hmm" Jacques sighed as he pulled off a bit of rough public bathroom toilet paper, "I find it hard to believe that you have a freak show in this bathroom. I think I'll..."

"IT'S NOT IN THE BATHROOM!" The voice shouted, interrupting Jacques, "DID I SAY IT WAS IN THE BATHROOM?!"

"Hey!" Jacques answered, "Calm down! I just assumed that you meant..."

"I asked if you wanted to see a freak show. No where did I imply that it was here in the bathroom."

"Well, I mean, you're waiting in the bathroom of a truck stop Burger King and whispering to random strangers at 3:30 in the morning. It doesn't really seem like there's anywhere you can take me, nor does it seem like you are going to actually find someone to go with you to a second location. That's why I initially thought that you were propositioning me in back water truck-stop code."

A moment of contemplative silence passed as the voice in the next stall thought about what it had just been told.

"I..." The voice stammered, "I guess I see your point. No, the freak show isn't here in the bathroom."

"So you DO expect strangers to go with you to a second location at 3:30 in the morning?" Jacques asked as he wiped himself clean.

"I guess so," The voice answered, "But it's not like I'm asking you to go far. It's actually really close by."

"Oh?" Jacques said as he pulled his pants up.

"Oh yea," The voice said, "It's just out back."

"Out back?"

"Yea. The entrance is out by the dumpsters."

"See," Jacques said with a laugh, "This is exactly what I mean! It REALLY sounds like you are trying to get me to go out back by the dumpsters where it is nice and dark so you can either kill me or fuck me. It's still off putting!"

Jacques reached back and flushed the toilet before he opened up the stall door and stepped out to the sinks where he began to wash his hands.

"So I'm sorry," Jacques said as he soaped up his hands, "But I am going to have to pass."

"I'm sorry to hear that." The voice said as Jacques shut off the sink, "You have no idea what you're missing out on. We have a bearded lady."

"A bearded lady, huh?" Jacques said as he stepped in front of the stall where the voice was coming from.

"Five, actually." The voice clarified.

"You're freak show has five bearded ladies?"

"It has as many bearded ladies as it needs, actually."

"Okay, see, you did it again. Comments like that are weird. Listen..." Jacques reached out and placed his hand on the top of the stall door in order to lean against it as he passed on his little tidbit of wisdom to the stranger in the bathroom stall, but as soon as he leaned his weight into it he found that the door wasn't locked and it flew open. Jacques looked into the stall aghast as he found it empty.

Void of any and all life, human or otherwise.

"Well." Jacques said to himself, "I guess I COULD go for seeing some bearded ladies..."

And with that, Jacques exited the restroom. With his bowels empty he felt a reinvigorated urge to experience the world as it happens, regardless of how silly it may be.

So a disembodied voice invited him to a freak show out by the dumpsters behind a truck stop Burger King, what of it?

It sounds intriguing.

***

Somewhere beyond the veil of the reality that we are used to hides a secret world that flat out refuses to allow us to understand the simple fact that it exists without us having a clear desire to learn about it. Knowledge is power, my friends, and it serves a much more important purpose than to simply make us aware of the world that we live in. It exists to help us to be human. It opens up our desires and helps us understand our limits. It forces us to place our world into the kind of nice little box that our primitive monkey brains crave, so that we can live out our lives in comfort that the world exists and that we get it.

But we don't get it.

Regardless of the vast amount of knowledge that the collective of our aforementioned monkey brains has acquired, the amount of knowledge that we remain blissfully unaware of is unimaginably vast.

The answers to our greatest questions remain a mystery to us. We have devoted centuries of academia for the specific purpose of answering these questions and we are still blind to the light that their answers might provide. And the worst part is that through all the years of asking these questions over and over again, we have been living within the answer itself. We just don't know how to conceptualize what it all means.

Where did we come from?

Where are we going?

Why are we going there and why did we come from where we came from?

The likelihood of us ever being able to understand the answers to these questions is all a matter of evolution. We simply aren't ready to get it yet. It's best to stick to the questions that we actually have a chance to answer.

What's behind the tarp that Jacques found draped between these two dumpsters behind Burger King?

Yes.

That will do.

"What the hell am I looking at?" Jacques asked aloud.

"Destiny." A voice answered, its intonation muffled by the ruffling of the nearby bushes that the source was clearly hiding behind.

As Jacques turned his attention to the bush he began to hear the sound of leaves rustling mixed with the unmistakable stamper of feet running away to hide in a new spot.

"Do not seek the source of the voice!" the voice called from somewhere beyond the bushes, "It will bring only misery if you look upon it!"

"What?" Jacques asked.

"My..." The voice stammered, "My true face will only bring you pain, for you are not ready to look upon it!"

Without having to look too hard, Jacques found the source of the voice. It was coming from just on the other side of the fence that the bushes sat beneath. As he pulled himself up and looked over the top, Jacques saw him. A frail, older man, bundled up under a red and black plaid blanket draped over his shoulders. On his head he was wearing a matching red and black plaid hunting cap, the ear warmers down, covering the sides of his head and doing their best to hide what Jacques could only assume were scars placed over the man's temples after some sort of invasive brain surgery. The man's chin jutted out in a way that showed he was either missing all of his teeth or suffering from a severe under-bite. Below his waist, he wore nothing. His dick and balls flopping in the breeze for all the world to see. Was this why he was hiding? Because he didn't want anyone to see his naked cock? Did he not want to have to explain the deep purple bruising lashed across his insignificant ass-cheeks?

"What happened to your ass?" Jacques asked, staring at the source of the voice and sending him into a fit of panic, scampering all about the small fenced in area where he was hiding.

The only way out was through the small hole where he had entered.

"Noooo!" He howled in a weak but otherworldly tone, "Noooo! Don't look at me!"

"Relax!" Jacques said, "I already looked at you."

The source of the voice scampered into the far corner of the pen that he found himself in and he collapsed. He pulled his knees into his chest, inadvertently pointing his asshole at Jacques and he began to weep.

"You weren't supposed to seeeeeee me!" He cried, "You were supposed to enjoy the shoooooow!"

"Listen, man," Jacques said, "I can still see the show. I still WANT to see the show. In fact, after seeing your face, I kind of want to see it more!"

"How could you?" he bawled, "Look what they did to me! Look what they did to my brain!"

The source of the voice pulled up the flaps on the side of his hat and showed his scars to Jacques. The scars weren't crude, they were placed with the precision of a surgeons hand, implying they were placed post-op.

"What happened?" Jacques asked.

"They took my dreams away!" The source cried, "They turned my sleep into darkness!"

"Who did?"

"The doctors." The source barked, his weepy sensibilities taking a back seat to the rage he seemed to feel for the subjects of his commentary, "Those god damned doctors."

"Why?" Jacques asked, "Why did they take your dreams?"

"They asked about them," He answered as he stood up, "they wanted to know about my head."

"Why?"

"Because my dreams are the things of wonder, sheriff."

"I'm… I'm not the sheriff…"

"And my daydreams will make you rethink life itself."

"Why did you call me sheriff?" Jacques asked.

The source looked Jacques from his toes to his face and back down again. With a twitch his glare shot quickly back to Jacques' face and a half smile stretched above his chin.

"I didn't know what else to call you." He answered.

"Well," Jacques said after a moment of thought, "You can call me Jacques."

Jacques held out his hand and the source took it in his own.

"Pleased to meet you Mr. Jacques," He said, "You can call me Marcel."

"Marcel…" Jacques took a moment, "Where is this freak show you promised me?"

"Why, it's just over here." Marcel said as he led Jacques to the tarp that was stretched between the two dumpsters, "All you have to do is step inside."

Now, Jacques considered himself a reasonably intelligent man. He certainly wasn't the smartest man out there, far from it, but he also wasn't the dumbest. He felt that in the grand spectrum of intelligence, he sat somewhere on the above average side of things, but still not to far from the middle. Hence the word reasonably being tacked onto the description of his intelligence.

A reasonably intelligent man should know better than to walk blindly into what could very likely be a dangerous situation. Should a reasonably intelligent person trust a weeping, pants-less man with surgery scars crisscrossing the parts of his skull where his brain is most accessible? No, of course not! The likelihood of getting bashed over the head as soon as you walk through that tarp and being removed of your wallet, watch, and anal virginity was higher than any reasonable person should be comfortable with.

But of course, intelligence isn't everything. Jacques curiosity currently superseded his base survival instinct. He wanted to know what this bizarre troll of a human was hiding back here. What had he hidden behind these dumpsters? He said he had a bearded lady.

No, he said he had FIVE bearded ladies.

No.

He said he had as many bearded ladies as he needed.

What did that mean? Why did he say that?

Who needs more than one bearded lady?

What respectable freak show needs multiple bearded ladies?

What respectable freak show sets up in a truck stop, behind the Burger King?

At three in the morning…

Despite a few red flags flapping right in his face telling him that it was a bad idea, Jacques pulled aside the tarp and stepped into the freak show.

Inside, dogs, all lying asleep beneath signs meant to indicate what they were. Under a sign that read Thumbalina slept a tiny chihuahua. Another sign reading 'The Great Western Giant' slept a large great Dane. And of course, in the corner, a sign that read 'Bearded Lady' hung above a German Shepard that was wearing a fake beard.

She was awake, and she was happy to have company.

She trotted over to Jacques and rubbed her head against his leg, Jacques reached down and gave her a scratch behind her ear as Marcel poked his head in through the tarp.

"I hope you are enjoying the show," Marcel whispered, "Can I bring you any more Bearded Ladies?"

Crucianelli
(Journal Entry c. 2019)

I watched a video today and I can't seem to get it out of my head.

A young woman, somewhere in her early twenties, is standing against an aging brick wall in a nondescript alleyway somewhere in Europe. She's alone and she's lovely. She seems unaware at first that she's being filmed as she expertly plays La valse d'Amèlie on the Crucianelli accordion that's hanging loose from her chest. She smiles brightly as soon as she notices the camera and its operator. She clearly knows who's filming her and seems to be happy to see them.

The whole situation is captivating. Her smile seems to transcend the situation as it reaches out through the screen and holds me tight and reminds me that I'm worthwhile. It helps me to feel feelings that I had forgotten I was capable of a long time ago. I feel as if for an instant, I get to feel the love that the one who's filming gets to feel on a daily basis, as if for a moment, I get to be someone else. Someone who's loved, and wanted, and cherished. I miss feeling like someone is happy to see me.

Then the video ends and the tranquility is washed away by a wave of lost thoughts and memories reminding me of all the years I missed out on. The future that I never got to look forward to.

I can only imagine what life could have been like if it had all played out differently. Maybe I could have been there, in that alleyway in Madrid or Rome or Paris or wherever it was, listening to the sounds of affection fingered expertly into an instrument I could never dream of learning to play; taking in smiles far more lovely than I've ever deserved.

Life could have been different.

I may never make it to Rome or Madrid or Paris or any of those old European cities that only seem to turn up in history books and romantic fantasies, but even if I do, I'll never get to be young again. I'll never experience the world that I never knew I wanted to see and I'll never get to experience what lies beyond the walls that my past spent my entire life hammering into me. The world's always been there. It's been waiting thirty seven years for me to get out there and experience it and I don't want to let it wait anymore.

I want a reminder that I'm more than a just a victim of circumstance.

I want to hear the music of the world and experience it as it plays out in front of me.

I want to get out there and experience the smiles of a world that's happy to see me.

The Way the Hills Dance

The dingy white truck sat with its turn signal clicking, waiting for a gap between the myriad of cars, trucks, and tractor trailers barreling down the highway, the golden autumnal hills of California surrounding it on all sides. Tim sat patiently, as he always did, remembering that the inopportune placement of his driveway was an easy trade off for the out of the way placement of his home and the beautiful scenery it sat within. Hilly California countryside in all directions, dancing to life with the cool breeze blowing through the air. Dancing in the way that only hills can. The truck itself was noisy; the engine needed a good lubing, the fan belts were all but cracking, and the dulcet sounds of The Beatles 'Revolution' was droning from the floor speakers that Tim had installed himself some ten years prior.

The people however, sat in silence.

When a break in traffic finally opened up, Tim took the opportunity to pull onto the pavement, kicking up a cloud of dust as his tires hurled rocks and dirt in all directions.

"Dad," Molly said, adding a human voice into the mechanical harmony, "Why do we have to go through this every week?"

"We've been doing this every week for almost two years now. You still feel the need to ask me every single time?"

"Well, just pretend I forgot."

"I'm thirty three years old Molly," he responded with a touch of sarcasm in his voice, "my days of Pretending are far behind me."

"Daaad." She whined.

"Fine. You know that you come over to my house every Friday after school, and I take you home every Sunday evening. It's called dual custody…"

"Another term concocted by liberal women lawyers to screw the man out of yet another one of his fundamental rights." she said with a mocking tone, clearly directed at her father.

"That isn't funny."

"Sure it is."

"…Kind of."

"So, where's the drop off point this time?" She asked.

"The McDonald's on La Playa Ave."

"The one that's like a block from Mom's house?" Molly interjected, "Why doesn't she just have you take me right to the house?"

"Even a sixth grader realizes the absurdity!" Tim exclaimed with a dry, sarcastic laugh.

"It's Bill you know."

"I know…"

"He's afraid of you, that's why he doesn't want you around. You know he doesn't think I should come over and see you on the weekends, he says you're a bad influence, but you know what, he's just a big, stupid, dickhead!"

"Molly!" Tim laughed, "Language!"

"He doesn't get why you live so far out of the way, or how you manage to live without a 'real' job." Molly continued, "I try to tell him that you're a published author, but he still doesn't understand how you get your money. He say's there's no way royalty checks for two books can sustain you."

"Three books." Tim said under his breath.

"That's what I say, but he never listens!" She felt herself getting worked up, "I just don't like him. I really don't like him."

"Easy now Molly," Tim said as he pointed the truck towards the drop off point, "we're here, don't let your mother see you all riled up."

The truck dipped as it eased its way up the entrance to the driveway of the McDonald's parking lot. Molly spotted her mother, standing outside of her Mercedes. The scowl on her face made the hairs on the backs of both of their necks stand at attention. Tim pulled the truck up next to her and slowly cranked the window down as Molly climbed out through the passenger door.

"Here Molly," Christine said as she handed Molly a ten dollar bill, "go get something to eat."

She turned her attention to Tim as Molly skipped off to the entrance to the restaurant.

"You're late, again." The anger in her voice could make a buzzard cry.

"We wouldn't have been if she didn't take her sweet ass time cleaning her room." Tim answered with a smile that he hoped would quell the tension of the situation.

"That isn't my problem!" Christine barked back, "The deal is 5:30, not 5:31, and definitely not 5:45!"

"I'm sorry Chris, It won't…"

"Don't call me that."

"*Christine*. I'm sorry *Christine*." Tim answered as the smile on his face washed away, "It won't happen again."

"If it happens again, I'm going to the judge to fix the arrangement," Christine warned, "this is unacceptable."

"It won't happen again" Tim assured her as Molly strolled up and stood next to her mother, chocolate milkshake in hand.

"Yea, we'll see, won't we?" Christine said, her voice dripping with derision, "Let's go Molly."

Much to her mother's chagrin, Molly climbed up the sidestep on drivers side of the truck and kissed her dad on the cheek. As she climbed down, she pulled out her change and smiled.

"Milkshake are two bucks, eight for me." She said as she slid the money into her pocket, "Best part is, she's to mad at you to even notice."

"Give her the change Molly." Tim called behind her as she walked away.

Molly turned around and placed her index finger next to her nose, a term of endearment between her and her father, something they have been doing for so long neither of them could remember where it started. As she opened the door to her mother's car, Tim mirrored the motion back at her. Molly climbed in and waved as she and her mother drove away. A serene smile perked back onto his face as Tim reached down to the ignition and shut down the engine.

"Two dollars is pretty good for a milkshake."

* * *

Christine's car was far more comfortable than Tim's truck. It was quieter, the seats were softer, and it smelled nicer. Molly would never let her father know that she felt this way, but she was well aware that he already knew. It's a brand new Mercedes, of course it's nicer than his thirty year old truck. Even still, she'd rather not bring it up.

As Molly began to fiddle with the power windows, the car was suddenly filled by the sound of Christine's phone's ringtone, the soft fluttery call of several songbirds tweeting to her attention the fact that she was receiving a phone call. The rough barking of Christine answering the phone provided a fine juxtaposition to the serenity that the birdsong had created.

"Yea?" Christine said as she held her cell phone up to her ear.

Molly listened to her mother's side of the conversation as she continued to slide the window up and down and up and down and up and down again. She knew she was talking to Bill. She could hear his voice. She hated his voice. She hated him.

"No," Christine said, "We'll be home in a minute."

Molly could hear his voice on the other end of the phone. She couldn't make out exactly what he was saying, but she could tell that he was upset.

"Yea, I know." Christine said, "I told him that if it happens again we're going to have to talk to the judge."

"You shouldn't talk on your phone while you're driving." Molly told her mother.

Christine scowled at Molly while the mumbled voice on the other end seemed to ramble on and on.

"Stop messing with the window!" Christine said, "You're going to break it."

"Oh please," Molly said in a snotty tone, "It's not going to break."

"Just cut it out!"

Molly pushed the button one last time to roll the window back up before leaning back in her seat and petulantly throwing her arms across her chest in hushed anger. She hated when her mother talked about her father. He was a good man and a great dad, a fact that Molly wanted to scream into her mother's face whenever she heard her and her so-called step father discussing him.

"No," Christine said into the phone, "she was messing with the windows... I know... I know, I told her... Yea, she's listening... He rubs off on her, sure, but when she's with me, his influence goes away..."

Molly found it funny how two people who supposedly hate her father can't seem to have a conversation without him being brought up. It's like he's living inside of their heads without paying rent. Not rent free, mind you, he just refuses to pay. Why *would* he pay? He doesn't want to be there, this is their problem. They're the one's who can't seem to think of anything else.

"I told him Bill, I told him that he can't be late again... Yea, I know, people are waiting... Yea," Christine laughed, "He tried to blame it on Molly. He said she..."

"You shouldn't drive while talking on the phone!" Molly shouted at her mother, interrupting her conversation, "You're gonna cause an accident!"

"Bill, I gotta go," Christine said, glaring at Molly, "Yea, love you too, I'll see you when we get home."

Christine hung up the phone as she pulled the car to a stop, the upcoming light turned yellow and she didn't want to risk it.

"Thanks mom." Molly said with a sarcastic tone.

"What's your problem?" Christine asked.

"I don't have a problem," Molly answered, "I just like not dying in fiery car crashes that are completely preventable."

"Oh stop it." Christine answered, "nothing was going to happen."

"Distracted driving is just as bad as drunk driving."

"I wasn't distracted!" Christine laughed as the light turned green and she eased the car through the intersection, "I was talking to Bill. It's no different than me talking to you right now."

"Bill's a distraction." Molly said, turning and looking out her window.

"What does that mean?" Christine asked, "How is he a distraction?"

"He just is."

Molly watched out the window as the familiar sites of her weekly ride passed by outside. The school down the street, the park at the corner, the house at the end of the cul-de-sac, and finally the bushes that flanked either side of her mother's driveway all passed in and out of her life as she made her way to the familiar new world that dual custody dictates she live in for the next week.

* * *

As Tim slid his key into the lock of his front door he could hear the distinct sound of his cat Foster tromping through the foyer and up onto the table that sits in the entryway. He could hear Foster pawing at the door and meowing as he paced about the small tabletop, knocking down several picture frames as he does any time someone comes to the door. As he stepped inside, Foster pawed at Tim's arm and mewed in excitement, happy that his best friend was home.

"Can't I come home one time without having to pick these up?" Tim said as he scratched Foster behind his ear

Tim set his keys down on the side table before bending down to the floor and picking up the frames. He smiled at Molly in the photos and set them down before heading into the house. As he made his way into the kitchen Foster rubbed his body in and out between Tim's legs, as excited cats are wont to do.

"Are you hungry?" Tim asked, "Let me get you some food."

Tim went to the pantry and fed Foster. He meowed a delighted meow before shoving his face into his bowl and eating his dinner. As

Tim went back to his bedroom to change his clothes, he heard a knock at his front door. He turned around and headed back to see who it was. Pulling the curtain aside, Tim peeked out through the front window of his house.

"Oh Christ." Tim said with disdain as he saw who was standing on his porch.

It was Mickey Greene, Tim's literary agent, and Tim knew this visit couldn't be good. The last time he had heard from Mickey he was told that if he didn't up his workload and get some pages turned in, the publishers were backing out of their deal. Sure, Tim had upped his workload. He had managed to start churning out page after page, day after day, of not entirely worthless, unusable crap.

Tim couldn't think of the last time anything he wrote stuck out to him. He had published three books, and even those were below Tim's lofty standards. Tim knew he could write. He had the published works and the sales record to prove that people liked what he did, but the reality of the situation was that Tim didn't like what he put out. He knew he could do better, and like any artist worth their salt, he had a vision in his head that he had been struggling his entire life to properly put down onto paper and failing at every turn.

He had a story to tell, he just couldn't seem to tell it.

"Mickey!" Tim said with a tenor of faux delight, "What, were you following me? I just got home!"

"No, nothing like that." Mickey replied as the two shook hands, "I was parked down by the highway. I got here about an hour ago but you weren't home, so I decided to wait and see if you might come back. I hope that's okay."

"It's fine," Tim said as he stepped aside and motioned for Mickey to come in, "Come on in."

Tim closed the door behind Mickey as he came in. Mickey followed Tim into the kitchen where Tim offered him a place to sit.

"Can I offer you a drink?" Tim asked, "A soda, a beer, something stronger?"

"No," Mickey answered, "I'm fine."

"Your loss." Tim said with a laugh as he grabbed himself a beer from the fridge, "So to what do I owe the pleasure of your company?"

"Well, Tim, it's the publishers."

Tim could have guessed as much.

"Well shit," Tim said as he popped open his beer, "Maybe I should have went with something stronger..."

"Well," Mickey laughed, "They've been getting your pages."

"That's good, right? That's what they wanted. Ten pages every week."

"Yea, yea, and they're happy with your work." Mickey said with a smirk, "Their concern is with your story."

"What's wrong with my story?" Tim asked as he sat down.

"Well," Mickey said, his tone turning serious, "They're concerned that the story isn't going to be scary enough."

"It isn't a scary story. I don't write scary stories."

"I know," Mickey assured, "that's what I told them, but they just kept saying that the story isn't scary enough. Too much family drama, not enough scary."

"Why do they think it needs to be more scary?"

"They seem to think that they're working with a horror writer." Mickey explained, "They're working with the guy who wrote a book called Ghosts in the Basement, they want more ghost stories."

"Ghosts in the Basement wasn't a ghost story!" Tim quietly shouted, "It was about a gay couple having to hide their love from the 1950's society they lived in! The title was a reference to their wives hearing them making love in the basement and assuming the house was haunted!"

"Is THAT what that book was about?" Mickey asked, excited.

"It's nice to know that you actually *read* my work." Tim laughed as he took another sip from his beer, "A real crack agent Mick, that's what you are!"

"What can I say? I'm not a big reader."

"And yet you decided to become a literary agent."

"The cards fell the way they fell my friend." Mickey replied, "It is what it is."

Tim smiled at Mickey and took another drink from his beer. He stood up from his seat and paced about the kitchen for a moment before Mickey piped up.

"So about the book…"

"Mickey," Tim said, fully aware of what Mickey was about to say, "if you tell me that I need to write a scary story, I'm not going to be happy with you."

"You need to write a scary story."

With an annoyed smile on his face, Tim took another swig from his beer and set the bottle down on the counter a little harder than intended.

"Mickey, I don't write scary stories."

"I understand that, Tim, but this is the situation. They already paid you under the assumption that you were going to be giving them a scary story that they can sell to teenagers. Maybe even something that they can sell to a movie studio to turn into a cheesy horror movie that can bank you a million dollars."

"But I don't write scary stories."

"But they think you do."

"And why is that?" Tim sarcastically shouted, "It's not like I have an agent or something who's job it is to sell me to the publishers based on the work I've done in the past."

"To be completely fair, I did sell you based on your prior work. They just made some assumptions that I wasn't aware of."

"Well isn't that nice."

"Tim," Mickey said, trying his best to sound reassuring, "You have two choices here. Give them their money back, or give them a scary story."

Giving the publishers their money back certainly wasn't an option. After the deal went through Tim decided that his house could use a fancy new patio where he could sit in silence and watch the hills around his home dance their majestic dance. It didn't use up his entire payment, but it wasn't exactly cheap. A good portion of what was left over was going into a college fund for Molly and the rest was for him to live in comfort for the next year or so.

Tim was going to have to bite the bullet here…

"Shit." He said as he finished the last of his beer, "I don't write scary stories."

* * *

The ceiling didn't seem to change. No matter how long Molly stared at it and no matter how hard she willed it, she simply didn't have the power to alter the shape of the ceiling by simply staring at it. It isn't as if she actually believed it was something that she'd be able to do, but it's better to be safe than sorry, right? The chances of her having telekinetic powers were pretty much zero, but that small sliver of a chance hidden in the percentages made it worth her time to find out. You never know unless you try, right?

"Molly!" Christine shouted from somewhere downstairs, "I'm not going to tell you again! Get out of bed!"

"I'm up mom, jeez!" Molly shouted back.

She wasn't up of course, not really. He mother asked her to get up about fifteen minutes ago and here she was, lying on her back, staring at the roof, testing out whether or not she had some sort of innate hidden abilities. No, she wasn't up in the sense that she was out of bed and getting ready for school the way she should be, she was up in the teenage sense of the word. That is to say, she was awake and she felt that was good enough.

"Get up Molly!" Her mother shouted, knowing full well that she was still in bed.

"I'm *up*!" Molly barked back as she threw her blankets off of herself and finally decided to get ready for the day.

Molly could smell the distinct scent of turkey bacon frying in a pan somewhere downstairs. It's always nice to wake up to something pleasant, and the smell of cooking turkey bacon was just that. Molly may complain about her mother a bit more than is necessary, but in reality she could never call her a bad mom. She has always been a kind and caring woman and Molly knew it, even if she did question her choices in regards to the people she chooses to spend her time with.

Christine and Bill married just two months after her divorce from Tim. As she got older, Molly had started to question the timing. How do two people come to the conclusion that they want to spend the rest of their lives together in just two months? Especially after one of the two had *just* decided to end it with someone that they had already promised to spend their life with. Relationships are a confusing concept to most twelve year old's and Molly was no exception. She doesn't understand the subtle nuance behind the reason why her parents split up, all she knows is that they did. She doesn't understand that they are better off apart, all she knows is that they aren't together anymore. It's a sad reality that she's forced to live in, but whether she realizes it or not, she's better off.

"Molly, if you keep lollygagging around you're gonna miss breakfast!" Christine shouted in her sternest voice.

"I'm coming mom!" she yapped back, "Just give me a minute, god!"

Molly threw on her clothes for the day. Normally she would take a little more time picking out an outfit, but today there's turkey bacon downstairs, fashion be damned. She'd already discovered that she doesn't have telekinetic power, there's no way she is going to miss out on turkey bacon and spend the day double-disappointed!

As she descended the stairs, Molly couldn't help but smile at the prospect of getting some of the deliciousness that was creating the savory fragrance that's been beckoning her downstairs more than her mother. Sure, its something small and mundane, but if we can't enjoy the small and mundane parts of life then how can we ever learn to appreciate the big ones?

"Glad you decided to join us." Christine said from her seat at the kitchen table, "Bill made breakfast, grab a plate."

Without missing a beat and maintaining her composure so as not to let he mother see the disappointment she was feeling inside, Molly walked right passed the food on the table and made her way to the pantry where she pulled out a box of pop-tarts.

"I'm running late," She said, "I'll just have a pop-tart."

"That's a shame." Christine said, "Bill worked hard on breakfast for us, maybe you should..."

"It's fine Christine," Bill interrupted, "She doesn't have time. I'll make her a plate for later, I'm sure it'll keep just fine in the refrigerator."

"Don't bother." Molly said as she opened up her pop-tart and headed out the door, "I'll be alright, see you after school mom!"

"You are being so rude right now!" Christine shouted to Molly as the door closed behind her.

Christine gave Bill an apologetic look as she helped herself to another piece of turkey bacon. She knew what Molly was doing. She knows Molly doesn't like Bill. Maybe she shouldn't have mentioned that Bill cooked, then maybe Molly would have sat down and ate breakfast with the family instead of rushing out the door with a growling belly and a fist full of empty calories. She doesn't blame her, of course, Molly's only twelve. Twelve year old's are blind to the things that take place outside of their own realm of understanding. No, Christine blames herself. She sprung her marriage to Bill onto Molly out of nowhere. There wasn't a wedding ceremony or anything, they just went down to the courthouse and got all of the paperwork out of the way so that they could get on with their lives together. She hadn't even considered Molly's feelings at the time and now she regrets it. There isn't much she would have done differently. There still wouldn't have been a ceremony. They still would have went to the courthouse and done it the easy way. The only thing that would have been different about it is that Molly would have been informed. Would that have guided Molly's present day feelings in any way? Probably not. Molly's a daddy's girl. Christine would have been in the wrong no matter how it went down. All that telling Molly would have done is helped to alleviate Christine's conscience here and now. But it's not like it matters, Christine can't change the past. All she can do is try and shape the future. She can't force Molly to like Bill.

But she sure can try.

"Why don't you pick her up from school today?" Christine said to Bill, "Maybe spend a little time with her. If she gets to know you, maybe she'll ease up a bit."

"I don't know Christine, don't you think she'll get along fine without me?"

"Sure she will," Christine replied, "but I would prefer you two to get along. For my sake."

Bill smiled at Christine as he took another piece of turkey bacon.

"If you really want me to, then I'll do it." Bill said as he took a bite, "I'll pick her up from school."

"Thank you hun," Christine said with a smile, "It really means a lot to me."

* * *

"Scary story." Tim said aloud to himself in a downtrodden tone, "How the fuck am I gonna do this."

Mickey's visit hit Tim like a ton of bricks. In case it wasn't made clear before, Tim doesn't write scary stories. It's not that he dislikes them, no, it's quite the opposite. Tim love's them. He grew up on R.L. Stine and Stephen King and he came to the conclusion a long time ago that while they inspired him to go and tell his stories, they set a bar that he was never going to reach. He's tried his hand at horror in the past and it just never worked out. He could only write the words 'And then the monster jumped out at him and roared really loud' so many times.

He clearly wasn't very good at it.

Horror wasn't for Tim because Tim didn't know scary. Tim knew depression. He knew brooding and wallowing and sludging his way through the human condition, but he didn't know scary. You might be thinking, 'How in the world can someone claim to understand the drudgery of living a human life and not understand scary?!' and to that, I will tell you this: Tim *does* know scary. He understands it completely, he just doesn't realize it.

"Meow."

Foster had astute cat senses. He always seemed to be aware of Tim's stress and he tried his best to make him feel better. Whether it be as simple as a purring rub against his leg, a playful batting at his shoelace, or begging incessantly for some more food, Foster seemed to always know what to do to remind Tim that he was needed.

"What is it Foster?" Tim asked, "I don't have time to dick around right now."

"Meow."

"Maybe later, I need to get some pages written and before that I need to figure out how to change what I've already written into a scary story."

"Meow."

"Yea, I guess you can sit on my lap while I write. As long as you don't go psycho and bite me."

"Meow."

Tim bent down and picked up Foster. He carried him into his office where he sat down at his desk and started up his computer. He placed Foster in his lap and scratched him on the chin before he leapt free from Tim's lap and ran full speed down the hallway to do whatever it is that cats do to pass the time.

"Fine." Tim called out, "I didn't want you in here anyway."

The constant blinking of the cursor on a blank white computer screen is perhaps the most daunting sight for a writer who is struggling through a bout of writers block. Tim didn't have writers block before last night, he was punching out page after page of a very personal story involving his life with his daughter Molly and it was pretty good if he didn't mind saying so himself. But after learning from his agent that the publishers were expecting something scary, any and all progress he had already made seemed to come rushing to a halt. The ideas stopped flowing, the words stopped coming, and the ever present depression started to kick in. Doubly so after remembering that they had already paid him and the money was spent.

Blending scary into the story he's been working on for months felt damn near impossible. His life with Molly wasn't scary. It wasn't something that he wanted to cheapen into silly scares and an atmosphere that simply doesn't fit. His only real choices now are to start over from the beginning, or to meld what he already has into a story he doesn't want to write.

Compromise is a part of life. We all need to deal with it at one time or another and now it's Tim's turn.

* * *

Molly liked school. She loved learning, she loved socializing, she even loved the building itself. She found the old world brickwork to be both aesthetically pleasing and conducive to a stress free school day. Keep in mind, she was still in middle school. The kind of cynicism that informs you that your school feels like a prison doesn't really seem to kick in until high school. Junior high at the earliest.

Molly was a fan of school and learning and friends and everything her days brought her. She was NOT a fan of her mother being late to pick her up. It doesn't happen as often as Molly says, she tends to exaggerate whenever she is complaining about her mother to her dad, but it does indeed happen more often than she would like and today was no exception.

One by one, Molly watched as each and every one of her friends and school acquaintances were picked up by their parents in a timely manner. She was fine, mind you, she'd come to expect her mother's tardiness. It was all a part of that teenage angst that was starting to shine through Molly's personality. Her mom was late maybe once every couple of weeks, but of course in Molly's mind that meant she was never on time. It's all a part of adolescence. At some point an incessant need for independence starts to tug at your pant-leg and beg you to let it free. But you're still a kid who hasn't learned how to deal with it so all you can manage to do is complain.

"Molly," Called a voice from somewhere behind her, "Do you need a ride home sweetheart?"

"Oh, no thank you." Molly answered, "My mom is picking me up, she should be here soon."

It was Mrs. Jansen, a kind older woman who worked in the school office and lived a few doors down from Molly's mom's house. Mrs. Jansen had given her rides before so it wasn't anything to worry about.

"Mind if I wait with you?" Mrs. Jansen asked, "I don't want you out here by yourself."

"I don't mind." Molly answered with a smile, "It's nice to have company."

"So how is everything?" Mrs. Jansen asked.

"Fine." Molly replied.

"How's your father? It feels like I haven't seen him in ages."

"He's fine," Molly replied, "he's working on his next book."

"Oh?" She asked, "That's good to hear. Do you know what this one is going to be about?"

"No," Molly answered, "He won't tell me. He says he's working with a new publishing house and he doesn't want to jinx it by letting the story get out there."

"He thinks you're going to let his story get out?"

"I'm pretty sure he's just messing with me." Molly smiled, "I wasn't around for his other books."

"Sure you were," Mrs. Jansen assured, "I remember it fondly, you were a chubby little baby."

"Well yea," Molly said, "I was alive, but I wasn't really around. He couldn't bounce idea's off me back then."

"Does he do that now?"

"Usually, yes," Molly answered, "but with his short stories and stuff. Not with this one. I don't know why."

"Maybe it's about you." Mrs. Jansen suggested.

"I never thought about that." Molly said with a thoughtful look on her face.

"I sure hope it is," Mrs. Jansen said, "I didn't much care for that last book. The one about the men having sex in the basement."

"Is *that* what Ghost's in the Basement is about?" Molly asked with a laugh in her voice.

"Oh," Mrs. Jansen said with a concerned look on her face, "I guess he wouldn't have wanted you reading that one. Don't tell him I told you that."

"I won't." Molly laughed before frowning when she noticed Bill driving her mom's car as it pulled into the school's parking lot.

"Look's like your ride is here." Mrs. Jansen said waving to Bill as he pulled up.

Mrs. Jansen headed off to her own car as Molly opened the door and climbed in with Bill. She sat down into the passenger seat and shut the door behind her.

"Your mom asked me to pick you up today." Bill said as Molly put on her seat belt.

"Okay."

"She said she would like us to get to know each other better."

"Okay."

"So how was your day at school?"

"Fine."

"Did you learn anything new?"

"No."

"So you just sat in class all day and learned nothing."

"Yep."

"Well alright then."

Bill shifted the car into drive and pulled out of the parking lot, heading off on to what was playing out to be a quiet drive home.

Molly sat silent in the passenger seat as Bill's phone began to ring.

"Hello?" Bill said as he answered the phone.

Molly could hear her mother's voice on the other end. She didn't know what they were talking about and she didn't care. The only thing that interested her right now were the car's power windows as she started to fiddle with them.

* * *

Tim stared at the white screen and the white screen stared back at him. Mocking him. Wordlessly reminding him that he's worthless. Utterly worthless.

This is exactly why Tim hates being accountable to someone else's ideas. When he's working alone he can allow himself to let his ideas flow freely. His creativity can be allowed to shine. When he's working under the whims of someone else his creativity gets stifled. The publishers want him to write something that he has never been good at writing. All it does is remind him of his shortcomings. It takes the fact that he can't do something and mushes it directly into his face and mocks him for it.

When the creative spark of an artistic mind isn't allowed to flourish it tends to fester into a bloated mess of depression and self doubt. Creativity can manifest itself in the most beautiful ways. The arts, writing, any act of imaginative creation represents the most basic idea of what separates us from the rest of the animal kingdom.

When our desire to express ourselves comes to a halt, we become no better than even the most basic of monkeys.

Without creativity we are nothing.

No one.

A mindless drone living in someone else's world.

"Meow."

"Good kitty." Tim said as he reached down and pet Foster on his fuzzy cat head.

"Meow!" Foster purred in delight.

Foster jumped up into Tim's lap and settled in. Tim turned back to his computer screen and sighed, it was like a wall of impossibility holding him back.

"Oh fuck this." Tim said as he placed his hands on the keyboard and started typing again.

Tim figured that his best bet was to keep writing the story that he wanted to write. Maybe something will come to mind as he goes that might make it fit what the publishers are looking for, maybe it won't. Tim is just going to write what he knows he can write and not cow tow to the ideas thrust upon him by an ignorant publisher who's whimsy is guided by an incompetent agent.

RING RING

Tim looked down to his phone to see who was calling. To his surprise he saw Christine's name plastered across the caller ID.

"That's weird…" Tim thought to himself, "Why would she be calling me?"

Christine can barely stand seeing Tim when he drops Molly off, why would she ever bother calling him.

"Oh shit…" Tim said as he realized that something must be wrong.

RING RIN…

"Christine?" Tim said as he answered the phone, "What's wrong?"

"Tim," Christine answered, Tim could hear the fear and trepidation dripping through her just saying his name, "Tim, there was an accident."

Tim's heart jumped into his throat.

"An accident?" Tim choked on his words, "Oh my god Chris, is Molly all right?"

"They're prepping her for surgery," Christine answered, Tim could hear that she was holding back tears, "Please get down here Tim, I'm scared, I need you."

"You need me?" Tim asked, scared and confused, "Where's Bill?"

"Bill's in surgery now." Christine answered, Tim could hear that she was crying, "Tim, I don't want to be alone."

"I'll," Tim stuttered, "I'll be there as soon as possible."

Tim hung up the phone and without a second thought he snatched up his keys and ran out the front door, leaving behind both Foster and his shoes.

* * *

Not many places are as cold and unforgiving as the daunting, not entirely sterile waiting room of a publicly funded hospital. Add to that the uncertainty of a loved one and the feelings of fear you're trying to repress boil over and manifest themselves as tears cascading down your face.

Christine's an ugly crier, she always has been. Whether she's crying for joy, sadness, or anger, her face was always the same, a scrunched up wrinkled mess bouncing up and down as she struggles to find a tempo to her breathing. But today is different. Christine's tears are coming from a place of fear and that fear is manifesting as simple tears running down a face that's as calm as an iced over pond on a quiet winter morning.

Tim was familiar with Christine's tears. A little too familiar. He had seen them in moments of joy and moments of anger. In moments of grief, and moments great frustration. But he had never seen them in a moment of fear. That's what made seeing Christine as he walked into the waiting room so disconcerting. Thinking back, Tim couldn't think of a single time he saw Christine scared. Despite their differences, Christine had proven a long time ago to be the strongest woman he had ever known, so seeing her now was something horrible, her head hung low with tears dripping from the end of her nose, the fear hiding behind the life in her eyes, it was all so terrifying. It meant that there was something to be scared of.

True terror.

Actual fear.

Tim felt a chill run down his spine as Christine looked up in his direction. Something in her eyes showed him that the situation was bad. The way she jumped up from her seat and embraced him in a hug told him that she was broken. This woman has wanted nothing to do with him since a year before their divorce when she cast him aside and started fucking Bill behind his back. Even before that, she was never a fan of hugging and other such sentimentality, so this here, now, was a clear sign that she wasn't just scared, she didn't know what to do.

"Chris," Tim choked out, "What's going on?"

"There was an accident." Christine answered, "A car accident. I heard it Tim. I heard the accident and there was nothing I could do."

"You heard it?" Tim asked.

"Bill called me to let me know the he picked up Molly when…"

"Bill picked her up?"

"I asked him to." Christine replied, "He was running late after work and wanted to let me know that he got her and I didn't need to worry."

"So he called you while he was driving."

"I heard it, Tim," Christine cried, "I heard the crashing metal, it was horrible!"

Tim squeezed her tight. He was livid at the situation but he knew this wasn't the time to bring it up.

"Where's Molly now?" Tim asked.

"Well," Christine said as she pulled herself away from Tim, "They took her back for surgery. That was about a half an hour ago."

"Surgery for what?"

"She broke her femur…" Christine started.

"The accident broke her femur, she didn't break anything." Tim broke in.

"Whatever…" Christine shot back.

"It's a distinction that needs to be made Chris," Tim said, "This wasn't her fault. We are going to need to make that clear to her."

"Why would she think it's her fault?"

"That's just how she is. She wants to take the whole world onto her shoulders and we need to make sure that she knows that its okay for her to rest."

"I know, I know," Christine replied, "Fine, the accident broke her femur so they are going to need to install a steel plate to hold it together."

"Is that common?"

"It's how they deal with broken femurs." Christine assured Tim.

"So it's something they do a lot then, good." Tim said as he started pacing around nervously, "We don't need to be too worried. Sure, I'm sure she's gonna need to relearn how to walk, but that's not too bad."

"There's something else, Tim."

"What is it?" Tim asked as he stopped pacing and looked back to Christine.

"She hit her head." Christine answered, "Hard."

"What?" Tim asked as tears started to well up in his eyes.

"Her brain is bleeding."

Tim didn't know how to react.

"They're going to need to go in and release the pressure that's building up." Christine added.

"Her…" Tim choked, "Her brain?"

"They assured me that the procedure is fairly basic and not as invasive as we might be thinking." Christine answered, "But as with any procedure, no matter how elementary, there is a chance for things to go wrong."

"What do you mean go wrong?" Tim asked, "Are you saying that she might die?"

"They say that it's highly unlikely."

"But the chance is always there." Tim replied as he sat down and placed his face in his hands.

"I know." Christine said as she sat down next to him and put her arm over his shoulder, "I know."

Together, Tim and Christine cried. They felt the uncertainty of their situation and they cried.

For their loved ones and for themselves, their tears were a release.

A guide to help them through this horrible moment.

* * *

Tim stared at his reflection in the window that sat across the waiting room and he screamed. Not out loud, mind you, in his head. A primal scream that encased every ounce of fear and anger and trepidation that he was feeling but couldn't outwardly express. He examined his reflection and he wanted to punch himself in the face. At this moment, he couldn't stand himself. Why wasn't he there? He could have prevented all of this if only he was there.

But he wasn't there.

He was at home bemoaning his chosen career path while his beautiful daughter was being rolled up into a pile of bent steel and broken bones. Her life is never going to be the same and there was never a god damned thing he could have done about it.

Christine was sleeping across several chairs under the window. Tim had draped his coat over top of her when he had noticed her shivering about a half an hour ago. She was exhausted, Tim could tell. He could see it in her eyes; they seemed lost and alone and scared.

Alone.

Tim stood up from his seat and walked to the empty nurses desk.

"Hello," He called out, "Is anyone here?"

There was no answer.

"Shit." Ted muttered to himself as he started to pace.

"Can I help you?" asked a woman wearing a set of purple scrubs carrying a clipboard.

"Um," Tim replied, "My daughter."

"Who is your daughter sir?" The woman asked as she stopped in front of Tim.

"She was in a car accident." Tim told her, "She has been in surgery."

"Of course." The nurse said with a concerned frown, "I'm sorry, I just started my shift."

"It's fine," Tim answered, "Is there any word yet?"

"None yet, but you and your wife…"

"Ex-wife." Tim corrected.

"Sorry," replied the nurse, "You and your ex-wife will be the first to know as soon as we hear anything."

"Of course." Tim said, lowering his head.

"Is there anything else I can do for you?" The nurse asked.

"Yes, um," Tim hesitated, "The man who was with my daughter…"

"I'm sorry," The nurse answered, "Like I said, I just started my shift…"

"It's fine," Tim said with a forced smile, "It's fine, thank you for your time."

He turned to walk away.

"Sir?" The nurse called out, noticing Tim's bare feet, "Would you like a pair of socks or something?"

"That would be lovely." Tim answered without looking back.

As he sat down he looked at Christine as she slept. She seemed off. She called him and told him that she needed him. She hasn't needed Tim's help in years. In all honesty, she *never* really needed Tim. The only reason she might need him is if she found herself utterly and completely alone and that made Tim sad. Where's Bill? Tim is far from Bill's biggest fan, but he makes Christine happy, and despite everything between them, Tim still loves Christine. Not in a relationship kind of way of course, but he cares about her. You don't dedicate as much of your life to someone as Tim had to Christine and simply forget about them. No matter how hard you try or how much you pretend its been completely snuffed out, the light's still there and it always will be. She may have broken his heart, but hearts mend, and forgiveness is easier than you might think.

"Sir?" The nurse called.

Tim turned to see what she wanted. She was carrying a pair of baby blue non slip socks.

"Thank you so much." Tim said with a smile as the nurse handed them to him.

"It's my pleasure." The nurse answered before heading back to her station.

Tim sat down and looked at the socks. The design in the non-slip material was fascinating to him. Was there something hidden in the design that he couldn't see? Was it just a random pattern splashed onto them haphazardly in some warehouse that could care less about the aesthetics of a pair of hospital socks that very few people would ever see, or was it patterned specifically to the human foot, maximizing the protected surface area and minimizing the potential for slip and falls? Tim slid the socks onto his feet without putting any more thought into their design. The answers didn't matter. There were more pressing concerns at hand.

As Tim pulled the socks onto his feet, he noticed a doctor coming through the set of swinging doors that lead to the sterile operating rooms. He was wearing a pair of clean scrubs as if he had just changed into them in order to look presentable before heading out into the waiting room to deliver some bad news. Tim stood up and his heart dropped as the doctor walked towards him. He was somewhat relieved when he continued walking passed him but his heart dropped again when he sat down next to Christine's sleeping form.

"My…" Tim stuttered, "My daughter…"

The doctor looked up at Tim.

"She is still in surgery," The doctor said with a half smile, "They are doing the best they can back there."

"So why…"

"I need to talk to her." The doctor said, motioning to Christine, "Alone."

The doctor gently shook Christine awake. Confused, having just been woken up, Christine took a moment to get her bearings. She looked around and slowly remembered where she was and why she was there. Any sense of serenity that her sleep may have granted her quickly slipped away.

"Ma'am," The doctor said as she started to wake up, "Can you come with me?"

Christine nodded as she stood up from her makeshift bed. She followed the doctor out of the waiting room, handing Tim his coat with an attempt at a smile as she walked passed.

The doctor led Christine out of the waiting room and into a small private room next door. Tim could see them through the window on the wall that faced the waiting room. He watched as he saw the doctor start to talk. Tim felt a rush shiver through his body as he saw Christine's hands shoot up to her face as the doctor continued speaking. Tim's heart dropped as he saw her begin to break down into tears. There was fear in her eyes. It was a look he had never seen in her before and it was upsetting. A look of absolute fear mixed with interminable grief and unbroken sadness. She fell into the doctor's chest and let out a scream that Tim could hear through the window. The doctor hugged her for a moment before helping her into a chair. He handed her some tissues and left through the door.

Tim felt a sense of confusion wash over him as the doctor began to walk in his direction.

"Sir?" The doctor said to him.

"Yea?" Tim answered.

"She asked for you."

"Oh." Tim answered, "Thank you."

The doctor made his way back through the swinging doors to the operating rooms as Tim walked and joined Christine in the private room the doctor had brought her to. Christine was out of sorts in a way that Tim had never seen before, crying and shaking. He sat down next to her and put his arm over her shoulder. She kept crying as she pulled in close to him and pressed her tear soaked face into his chest.

"Bill's dead." She managed to blurt out through her tears.

"Oh my god, Chris," Tim said as he held her tight, "I'm so sorry."

Christine continued to cry and Tim continued to hold her close. He couldn't imagine what she was going through right now.

"Is there anything I can do for you?" Tim asked, not knowing what else to say.

"Just," Christine managed through her tears, "Just stay with me. Please."

Tim held her tighter.

"I'm not going anywhere." He assured her.

"Please don't let me be alone…" She cried out to Tim, breaking his heart all over again.

* * *

The whir of electricity flowing through the caustic white neon lights overhead seemed to penetrate deep into Tim's brain. The hum mixed itself together with the light of the room itself to wash over him and penetrate every orifice of his being. The world around him wasn't his world anymore. It was something different, something new. A place of ambivalence where his every step would be held accountable to the whims and whimsy of the very people that were changing it all.

He stared at the coffee machine for some time. Vanilla, hazelnut, regular, decaf, cream, sugar, who gives a shit? All he needs is something to keep him awake for another twenty minutes of panic, fear, and confusion before he'd start to feel his eyelids get heavy and go spend another fifty cents on more filtered black uncertainty.

Plain black coffee. Tim punched in the proper command and the machine hummed to life. The sounds of swirling liquid filled the air, quickly drowning out the electric whir from overhead. It might have been startling had this not been Tim's third trip down the hall to the coffee machine. Or was it his fourth? Time was starting to slip away from Tim's perception but he was barely cognizant enough to notice. Staying awake was starting to get tough but he had no other choice. He needed to stay awake. He needed to stay strong. Everyone's sanity was sitting on his shoulders right now and it took every ounce of his being to remember that the world outside of his head was counting on him.

His cup dropped and filled with coffee and as if simply going through the motions, Tim picked it up and drank it down. It was as if the heat meant nothing to him. Or he simply couldn't feel it. He crushed the paper cup in his hand and as he threw it into the trash can something caught his eye. Sitting in the trash can, right next to where he had tossed his trash, sat a McDonald's cup, the remnants of the milkshake it once contained dripping from its lid.

"Two bucks…" He said under his breath to nobody.

Would she still like milkshakes?

Would she even remember what milkshakes are?

Would she be able to communicate her love for milkshakes to anyone?

Would she be able to communicate her love to anyone?

Would she be able to love?

Would she be able to *be* loved?

A tear rolled out of Tim's eye as he thought about the fact that his sense of uncertainty pales in comparison to the fact that his daughter didn't even know how uncertain her future was.

If she even gets a future.

Tim stared at the milkshake cup as his head filled up with horrible thoughts about a future that he had no control over. The electric whir spilling out of the lights overhead engulfed him once again and closed him off to the world around him. His vision narrowed down as his peripherals shone white with the corrosive glare of the neon light that he was bathed in. In that moment, his world consisted of naught more than a pile of garbage and the possible loss of a child.

He stared intently at that cup and couldn't seem to look away. Everything that was wrong with his world was right there in that crumpled pile of fast food cast off. Thought's of torment and disdain washed through his aching brain as he tried to take account of everything that may and may not go wrong in the immediate future. An hour from now, Tim could be father to a broken husk of the daughter he once knew. Conversely, everything could go right and she can be perfectly fine, save some steel screws in her leg and a bitchin scar on her head, but focusing on the positive felt like an impossibility right now.

Tim was startled when the electric whir over his head was suddenly interrupted by the familiar sound of his cell phone ringing in his pocket. Without any sense of emotion he pulled it out and looked at its face.

"Fuck…" Tim said as he saw Mickey's name splashed across the screen.

Tim chose to ignore the call and it started to ring again almost immediately.

"God damn it!" Tim shouted as he chose to answer it, "Mickey, this is a really fucking bad time to be calling me."

"Timmy," Mickey said, "This is important."

"It can wait." Tim answered as he hung up.

It immediately began to ring again.

"Mickey," Tim shouted, "This is a bad fucki…"

"They're dropping the horror angle!" Mickey shouted before Tim could finish.

"What?" Tim asked.

"I talked to the publishers and they said they don't need horror anymore."

Tim laughed to himself. These past several hours of living out his worst nightmare had driven him to a certain point where he felt that he really understood what horror could be. He watched someone he loved cry as she was given the news of losing her husband. He experienced the horror of not knowing what might come next. He learned that horror isn't what he had always thought it was and despite not realizing it just yet, he was in a place where he could finally give the people guiding his world what they wanted and now he is getting the news that he doesn't have to.

No.

No, fuck that.

"They'll get what they get." Tim said as he hung up on Mickey and shut his phone off.

With force, Tim shoved his phone back into his pocket as he looked back to the milkshake cup in the garbage. Positivity wasn't where his brain was right now, and frankly it wasn't where it needed to be. He needed to ready himself for the worst because if it turns out that this all ends up being even slightly better than the worst case scenario, he will have something to be thankful for. He will always be able to say that it could've been worse.

"Sir?" Came the familiar voice of the on call nurse from behind him, "The doctor's ready to speak with you."

Tim looked back at her and nodded. She smiled at him before leaving him be. He took a deep breath before heading back to the waiting room.

Before he stepped out he turned and took one last look back at the milkshake cup in the garbage can.

Two dollars is pretty good for a milkshake.

Right?

* * *

The waiting room was cold. Cold and seemingly devoid of all of the human emotion that makes most rooms easy to sit in. Four walls, a window, and a door were all there was to help curb the fear that hospitals tend to pull out of the people visiting them. Whether you're there for an emergency, a standard treatment, or a simple checkup, there is always that little tinge of fear hiding in the back of your head and tugging at your hair to remind you that something could go wrong. Hospitals are havens for disease and just being there can be a hazard to your health.

Waiting rooms are nothing more than human storage closets. A place to shove away the fear and trepidation that permeates through any standard hospital visit and let it fester into a swollen ulcer that will always stay moments away from bursting out into a rash of unadulterated skepticism and negativity.

We get four walls to hold it back. Four walls to remind us that for most of us, this is all just temporary.

Christine was still crying. She was trying her damnedest to hide it, but Tim could tell. The swelling in her eyes was a dead giveaway and the trails of mascara down to her chin did nothing to help camouflage it.

She had no reason to hide it. She didn't need to stay strong for anyone anymore. Her world was coming down right now. Nothing is ever going to be the same again.

'You are being so rude right now!'

The words kept running through Christine's head. It was the last thing she said to Molly before she left for school and for all she knew, those could be the last words she ever says to her daughter. Not something assuring, not 'I love you', not even a nice good bye. 'You are being so rude right now!'. Thinking about it did nothing but force out a new stream of tears for her to try and hide.

Tim sat down next to Christine and placed a reassuring arm over her shoulder. She looked up at him and tried to smile but all that came were more tears. He pulled her closer and she was grateful. She leaned her face into his shoulder as he squeezed her tighter. Regardless of how it all turned out between the two, no matter how they have come to feel about each other, they were all they had right now and they both knew it.

As the doctor stepped into the room, Tim could feel Christine tense up. Her body started to bob as her breathing became labored and full on panic began to set in. Tim knew she was anticipating the worst so he tried to reassure her with a gentle squeeze to let her know that they were in this together. She looked at him and Tim could see his reassurance meant nothing in that moment. She tried to compose herself but it was useless.

"Well," Said the doctor, "She made it through"

Neither Tim nor Christine knew how to react. They had both been preparing for the worst and still weren't sure if that was what was coming. In some situations, dead is better than broken.

"She is still asleep right now," The doctor said with a smile, "But we're confident that she is going to make it through."

"So," Tim piped up, "Does that mean we can see her?"

"Like I said," The doctor answered, "She's still asleep. We would like to monitor her until she wakes up, but I can take you in to see her."

"She…" Christine finally spoke up, "She is for sure going to wake up?"

"She is." The doctor said with a smile.

"And we can see her?"

"You can," The doctor answered, "But keep in mind, she was in a car accident. She's alive, she's breathing, and we managed to stop all of her bleeding and she is going to get through this, but seeing her might be shocking. She's been in surgery for nine hours, that takes its toll on a body."

"I…" Christine stuttered, "I just need to see her breathe."

* * *

The sight of Molly's broken body was almost too much for Tim to bare. He felt the tears behind his eyes begging to be set free and he almost granted their wish when he saw her swollen face. The bruising behind her eyes colored her skin a grotesque mixture of purple and yellow, her hair was gone, shaven perfectly clean save a six inch scar, stitched together with precision at the top of her head. She was covered in scrapes and bruises of varying shapes on every piece of exposed skin. It was all just so much. Too much. Shit, Tim knew it was even worse than it looks because he knows that under the blankets, Molly's broken leg has a huge stitched up scar hiding a broken femur held together by medical grade steel.

Tim felt the tears start to well up again but he forced them back. He fought them off because he needed to stay strong. He needed to stay strong for Christine. A woman who on any other day would hate his guts. A woman who by all rights, he should hate right back. But empathy doesn't work that way. It has nothing to do with the person and everything to do with the situations they might find themselves in.

Christine couldn't hold back her tears. The second she saw Molly she lost any and all sense of nuance and nearly broke down completely. She let out the kind of wail that you only hear coming from a grieving mother, blaringly loud and dripping with grief as if coming straight from the deepest, most pain ridden part of her entire being. The sight of Molly in such a broken state was far too much for her to handle and her knees began to get weak. Tim helped her to stay on her feet, but she wasn't making it easy.

"I told you," The doctor said as he tried to help calm Christine down, "She isn't easy to look at, but you need to remember that she is alive. She is going to make it through this. She's a strong kid."

His words did very little to ease her tension.

"You said you wanted to see her breathe Chris, and there she is," Tim assured her, "She's breathing. Look at her chest. She's breathing."

Christine nodded. She could see that Molly was breathing and that was all she needed. It did little to curb her tears, but it was still enough.

"I'm," Christine stuttered, "I think I need to leave this room."

The doctor nodded and helped her to the door. The tears were still falling hard from Christine's face, but she had managed to compose her self a bit. She just needed to not look back. She needed to not see Molly laying broken in that bed.

"I'm going to hang out in here for a bit," Tim said as they passed him, "If that's okay."

"Of course." The doctor said, ushering Christine back to the waiting room.

Tim smiled as they left him and he turned back to the window that was looking into Molly's recovery room. It was tough, but he was eventually able to see his daughter somewhere in the mangled mess that used to be her body. He could see her smile, hear her voice, feel her love. It was all there, it was just all hidden behind the muddled situation they found themselves stuck in. Once he could see through the facade that her condition presented, Tim found contentment. He realized that no matter what life threw in her way, she would always be Molly. Tim knew she was strong and he believed in her. Nothing short of Molly herself was going to take her down. She is such a strong girl. He was so proud of her.

Then Tim saw her start to stir. Molly was waking up. Tim watched and saw her slowly start to open her eyes. He watched as she blinked her eyes into focus and started to take in the room around her. She slowly started to move more, little by little. The pain he could see she was experiencing broke his heart and the confusion on her face nearly ripped it straight out of his chest.

Tim could see her try and speak but he couldn't hear her. He knew she was scared. He waved his arms above his head to get the nurse's attention and pointed to Molly to show her that she was awake. The nurse called for the doctor and rushed to Molly's side to talk to her and try to ease her confusion. Tim watched Molly wince with pain as she started to cry at the news of the accident and the surgery. Tim watched as she lifted her hand to her bald head and started to cry at the lack of hair. A tear fell from Tim's eye but he kept his composure about him.

The doctor soon entered the room. He stood next to her bed and began to speak to Molly. Tim couldn't hear them, but he assumed that he was telling her about the procedures and about the extent of her injuries. Tim watched as Molly's face went from fear to realization to hope. She was still crying but Tim could see that she wasn't as broken as she looked.

As the doctor left the room, Molly's gaze dropped down towards her lap. The nurse returned to her side and began to fiddle with her IV bag. She said a something to her that caused Molly to look up towards Tim.

Through her tears, Molly smiled. She placed her index finger next to her nose.

Through his tears, Tim did the same.

* * *

Tim typed away at his keyboard as if the word's 'Writer's Block' had lost all meaning. The words were flowing through his fingers and onto the screen at a breakneck pace. Paragraphs were flowing out followed by pages followed by chapters. Not only had Tim finally found his groove, he found his story. The story he has been writing for his entire life. He felt like nothing could stop him.

DING DONG

Almost nothing.

Tim finished up the sentence he was on and got up to go answer the door. Foster scampered in front of his path, enticed by the sound of the doorbell. He leapt up onto the side-table near the door and waited for Tim to open it so he could greet whoever it was with a forced head rub. As Tim peeked out the window to see who was there, he smirked and opened the door.

It was Mickey Greene.

"Hey there Mick," Tim said with a smile, "To what do I owe the pleasure."

"Do I sense a touch of sarcasm?" Mickey asked, "Because I assure you I come with good news."

"No sarcasm at all," Tim smiled back, "I am feeling so good right now that even your ugly face can't change my mood."

"Well that felt like an unnecessary jab," Mickey replied with some distaste in his mouth, "But I guess I'll let it slide."

"The only reason you think it's unnecessary is because you don't have to look at you." Tim said as he stepped aside and let Mickey in.

"I have to look at myself every morning," Mickey laughed, "Trust me, I know where you're coming from."

"Come on," Tim said, laughing and motioning for Mickey to follow him, "Let me get you a drink."

Mickey followed Tim into the kitchen. Tim walked to the fridge and pulled out two bottles. He popped them open and handed one to Micky who gratefully took it.

"So," Mickey said, "I was talking to the publishers and they…"

"Do you want to talk outside?" Tim interrupted, "Out on the back porch. It's nice out, the perfect evening for a beer, a sunset, and good friends."

"Sure," Mickey answered, somewhat taken aback, "That sounds nice."

Mickey followed Tim out to the back porch. The backyard was nothing to write home about, but you couldn't beat the view. Tim's fancy new porch bordered what seemed like miles and miles of lush California hillsides. There were homes here and there dotting the landscape, but they did nothing to diminish the beauty of it all. Tim pulled out a couple of simple plastic deck chairs and handed one to Mickey. The two sat down and took a moment to take in the scenery.

The hills danced in the breeze.

"This really is beautiful." Mickey said.

"This is what three books'll get you!" Tim laughed, "I'm hoping the fourth will land me some nicer deck chairs!"

"These are fine!" Mickey said, looking down at the plastic chair he was sitting in, "They remind me of the kind my mom had!"

"Well they may massage your nostalgia muscles," Tim laughed again, "But just give them twenty minute, your back will be begging for some padding!"

"Ah they're fine!" Mickey grumbled.

"You'll see." Tim smiled as he took a sip from his beer, "Deck chairs. Four books and some nice deck chairs. What else could I ask for?"

"Speaking of four books," Mickey said as he finished taking a drink from his beer, "Like I was saying before, I was just speaking with the publishers. They said that you could have an extension. They pushed your deadline back."

"I didn't ask for that." Tim said, leaning forward in his seat.

"Well," Mickey replied, "I spoke to them and we all agreed that you have been through a lot these passed few months and because of it, they're going to give you break."

Tim sat back in his seat again and took a drink from his beer. He crossed his leg over his lap and he looked at Mickey and he laughed.

"I appreciate that Mick." He finally said.

"I figured it was the least I could do. I owe you so much, you have kept me on as your agent for way longer than you should have and I really wanted to show you that I could…"

"I really do appreciate it Mick," Tim reiterated, "But I don't need it."

"You don't need it?" Mickey asked with a confused look on his face.

"Nope," Tim laughed as he drank from his bottle again, "I'm pretty much finished with it.."

"You're finished?!" Mickey said, leaning forward with a look of surprise slapped across his face.

"Yep," Tim replied with pride, "Just need to finish up the ending, give it a quick edit and it'll be good to go."

"That's," Mickey leaned back and smiled, "That is some of the best news I have heard in a while."

"I'm glad to hear it!" Tim laughed.

The two sat on the porch and drank their beers and watched the hills in the distance. The grass continued to dance in the breeze.

"Hey," Mickey said, breaking the silence, "You know what?"

"What's that?" Tim asked, still watching the hills.

"Remember when you sarcastically called me a crack agent because I didn't read your books?"

"Of course I remember," Tim laughed, "I think about it every day!"

"Well," Mickey continued, "I sort of took that to heart and I've been reading the pages you've been sending the publishers."

"Oh yea?" Tim asked, somewhat surprised, "That's great Mickey, I appreciate it."

"Well," Mickey said with a sense of sadness washed over his face, "After reading it, I understand why you were so adverse to writing a scary story. This book is going to be good. Too good to muddle up with a bunch of horror nonsense. This story is real. People are going to relate to it. It's really going to be something you can be proud of. The publishers agree."

"Well thanks, man." Tim said, turning to smile at Mickey, "That really means a lot to me."

"But I have to ask you something."

"Whats that?" Tim asked.

"Well you said you're finished with the story, right?"

"I am."

"Does the girl make it?" Mickey asked, his face filled with distress, "After the accident I mean, does she make it?"

"She makes it." Answered a voice from behind them.   Mickey turned to see Molly standing in the doorway, she was pushing her walker over the threshold and coming to join them on the porch.

"Hey sweetie," Tim said, standing up to help her, "What's up"

"Mom called," Molly answered, vigorously swatting away her father's attempt to help her, "She says she isn't going to make it to dinner. Something about meeting friends somewhere, blah blah blah, I didn't listen."

"You didn't listen?" Tim laughed.

"You know how she drones on and on," Molly answered as she gingerly lowered herself into the seat her father just vacated, "She's going out with her friends, that's fine. She deserves it."

"That she does." Tim answered as he pulled out another chair and sat down.

"Besides," Molly continued, "We were gonna barbecue. She thinks its all just empty calories. She wouldn't have eaten it anyway!"

"This is true." Tim said, "I just wanted to check up on her is all. It's been a while and I wanted to make sure she's okay."

"She's fine," Molly said in that oh so recognizable teenage tone before turning her attention to Mickey, "Hey!"

"Hey." Mickey replied somewhat uncomfortable.

"Why don't you stay for dinner?"

"I…" Mickey stuttered, "I don't know…"

"That's a great idea Molly," Tim said before turning his attention to Mickey, "Stay for dinner. Christine isn't coming. You can't expect the two of us to eat everything."

"Plus," Molly added, "You kind of have to stay."

"Why is that?" Mickey asked with a smile.

"Because I invited you," Molly replied, "And I almost died in a car accident that killed the driver. You aren't allowed to say no to me."

Mickey was taken aback. He looked to Tim for some guidance as to where to go from here.

"She's right," Tim laughed, "You can't say no to her."

Mickey smiled to them both and nodded, agreeing to stay for dinner.

"Good." Molly answered, "I don't know what I would do if I had to spend another dinner eating alone with this man."

Molly shot a smile at her father before standing herself up and waddling back into the house.

Tim smiled as he watched Molly leave. He leaned forward towards Mickey and held his bottle up.

"Life is beautiful, Mick," Tim smiled, "Try not to let it get in the way."

The two clanked their bottles together and leaned back into their chairs. They went back to watching the hills dance in the way that only hills can.

151

About the Author

Daniel F. Creeden Jr.

Born on a mountain top in Tennessee
Greenest state in the land of the free
Raised in the woods so he knows every tree
Kilt him a b'ar when he was only three

Wait…

No…

That was Davey Crockett.

Dan didn't do any of that.

He loves bears…

Praise for the author

Have you seen what this guy is packing? I've seen it, it really is a sight to behold.

-Dan Creeden Jr.

Did he imply that he has a big dick? Yea, no, don't listen to him. That guy is all balls.

-Erik Creamer

Book's over. Stop reading...